# A Treasury of

# CLASSIC STORIES

Bath · New York · Cologne · Melbourne · Delhi
Hong Kong · Shenzhen · Singapore · Amsterdam

This edition published by Parragon Books Ltd in 2014
Parragon Books Ltd
Chartist House
15–17 Trim Street
Bath BA1 1HA, UK
www.parragon.com

Edited by Laura Baker
Designed by Claire Brisley and Duck Egg Blue
Production by Joanne Knowlson

ISBN 978-1-4723-2712-3

Printed in China

# CONTENTS

# ALICE IN WONDERLAND

Alice was beginning to get very tired of sitting by her sister on the bank and of having nothing to do. It was hot, which made her feel very sleepy and slow. She was considering whether the pleasure of making a daisy-chain would be worth the trouble of getting up and picking the daisies, when suddenly a White Rabbit with pink eyes ran close by her.

There was nothing so very remarkable in that; nor did Alice think it so very unusual to hear the Rabbit say to itself, "Oh dear! Oh dear! I shall be too late!" But when the Rabbit actually took a watch out of its waistcoat pocket, looked at it and hurried on, Alice realized that she had never before seen a rabbit with either a waistcoat pocket, or a watch to take out of it. So she ran across the field after it and was just in time to see it pop into a large rabbit hole.

In another moment, in went Alice after it. The rabbit hole went straight on like a tunnel and then dipped suddenly down, and Alice found herself falling into what seemed like a deep well. It was too dark to see where she was falling to, but she could see that the sides of the well were filled with cupboards and bookshelves. She picked a jar labelled 'Orange Marmalade' from one shelf. Sadly it was empty, so she put it back.

Down and down she fell. There was nothing else to do, so Alice started thinking about her cat. "Dinah, my dear, I wish you were down here with me!"

Alice felt that she was dozing off and had just begun to dream, when suddenly, thump! Down she came on a heap of dry leaves, and the fall was over.

# ALICE IN WONDERLAND

Alice jumped to her feet and saw the White Rabbit hurrying down a long passage ahead of her. There was not a moment to be lost. Away went Alice like the wind, just in time to hear it say, "Oh my ears and whiskers, how late it's getting!" as it turned a corner. Then it disappeared from view.

Alice was now in a long, low hall with doors on all sides. They were all locked. In the centre of the hall was a little, three-legged glass table, with a tiny golden key lying on it. It didn't fit any of the doors, but then Alice saw a low curtain that she had not noticed before. Behind it was a little door, only forty centimetres high. She tried the little golden key in the lock. It fitted!

Through the door Alice could see the loveliest garden with bright flowers and cool fountains. How she longed to walk in it, but she could not even get her head through the doorway.

Feeling sad, Alice shut the door and went back to the glass table, only to find that a little bottle had appeared. Around its neck was a paper label with the words 'Drink me' on it. Alice hesitated a moment, but then took a sip. It tasted of cherry tart, custard, pineapple, roast turkey, toffee and hot buttered toast, and Alice very soon finished it off.

"What a curious feeling!" said Alice, as she shrank to only twenty-five centimetres high. Now she could fit through the little door into the lovely garden, but, alas, the key was still on the glass table, and she was much too small to reach it. Then her eye fell on a little glass box lying under the table. Inside was a very small cake with 'Eat me' written on it. Alice took a bite and then another until she finished it and had grown all over again.

# ALICE IN WONDERLAND

"Curiouser and curiouser!" cried Alice. "Goodbye, feet!" She looked down, and her feet seemed to be almost out of sight. At the same time, her head struck against the roof of the hall. In fact, she was now more than three metres high! She took up the little golden key and hurried off to the garden door.

Poor Alice! It was as much as she could do, lying down on one side, to look through to the garden with one eye; but to get through was more hopeless than ever. She sat down and began to cry. And though she tried to stop herself, she went on crying, shedding litres of tears, until there was a large pool all around her, about ten centimetres deep.

After a time, she heard a little pattering of feet in the distance. It was the White Rabbit returning, splendidly dressed, with a pair of soft, white leather gloves in one hand and a large fan in the other. Alice called out, "If you please, sir," which frightened the Rabbit so much that he jumped violently, dropped the gloves and the fan and scurried away as hard as he could go.

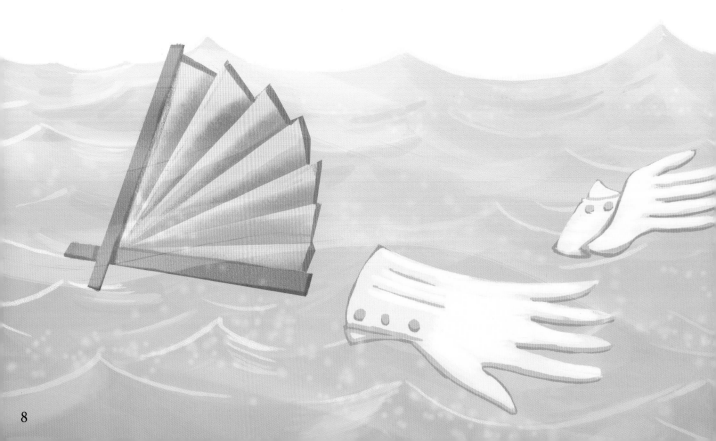

Alice took up the fan and gloves. The hall was very hot, so she fanned herself again and again. When she looked down at her hands, she was surprised to see that she had put on one of the Rabbit's little white gloves. "I must be growing small again," she thought. She dropped the fan hastily, which she realized was the cause of her shrinking, just in time to avoid disappearing altogether.

Suddenly, her foot slipped, the gloves went flying and splash! She was up to her chin in salt water, the gloves floating beside her. At first she thought that she had somehow fallen into the sea, but she soon made out that she was in the pool of tears that she had wept when she was three metres high. "I wish I hadn't cried so much!" said Alice, as she swam to the shore and then did her best to get dry.

# ALICE IN WONDERLAND

In a little while, the White Rabbit appeared again. "Where can I have dropped them, I wonder?" he muttered anxiously. Alice guessed that he was missing his fan and gloves.

Then the Rabbit noticed Alice and called out to her in an angry tone, "Mary Ann! Run home this moment and fetch me a pair of gloves and a fan!" Alice was so much frightened that she ran off at once in the direction he pointed to.

"He mistook me for his housemaid," she said to herself as she ran.

Soon she came upon a neat little house with 'W Rabbit' engraved on a bright brass plaque beside the door. She went in, hurried up the stairs and found a table in the window with a fan and a pair of tiny white leather gloves on it. She took them up and was just going to leave, when her eye fell upon a little bottle near the looking-glass. Alice uncorked it and put it to her lips. Before she had drunk half the bottle, she found her head pressing against the ceiling and had to stoop to save her neck from folding over. She went on growing, and, as a last resort, she put one arm out of the window and one foot up the chimney.

After a few minutes, the White Rabbit came to the door and tried to open it, but Alice's elbow was pressed hard against it. He then decided to climb in through the window. "That you won't!" thought Alice, and she waved her hand about. There was a little shriek as the Rabbit fell off his ladder.

The next moment, a shower of little pebbles came rattling in at the window. As Alice watched, they turned into little cakes. In the hope that eating a cake would make her smaller, she swallowed one and was delighted to find that she began shrinking. As soon as she was small enough to get through the door, she ran out of the house and away as fast as she could.

# ALICE IN WONDERLAND

Alice soon found herself in a thick wood and began searching for something to eat or drink to make her grow again. There was a large mushroom near her, about the same height as herself, and when she had looked under it, on both sides of it and behind it, it occurred to her that she might as well see what was on top of it. She peeped over the edge, and her eyes immediately met those of a large, blue caterpillar, sitting with its arms folded.

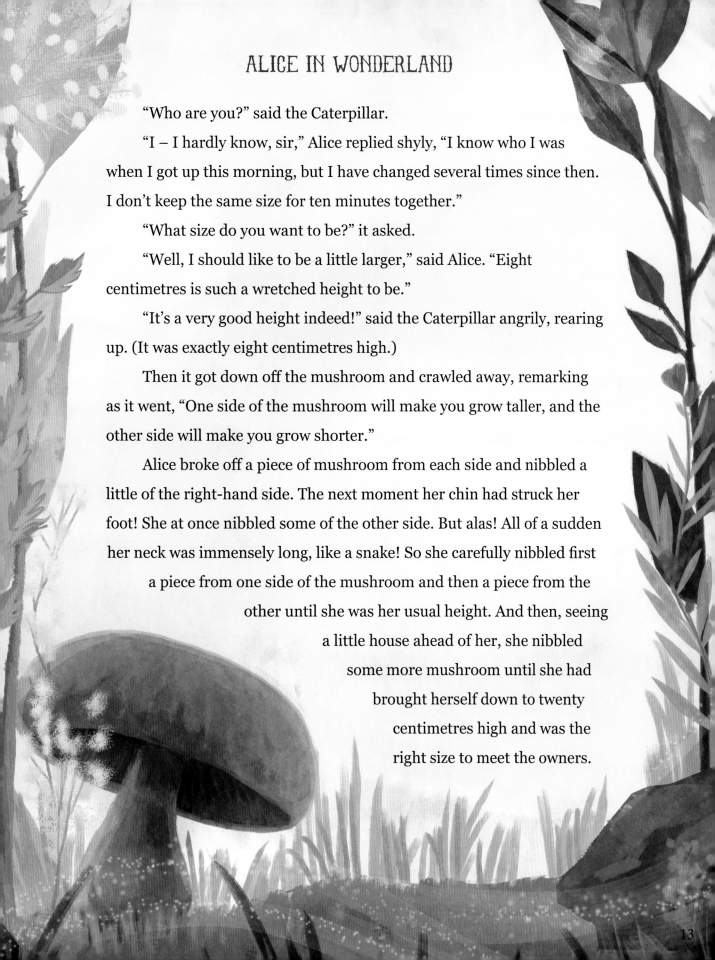

# ALICE IN WONDERLAND

"Who are you?" said the Caterpillar.

"I – I hardly know, sir," Alice replied shyly, "I know who I was when I got up this morning, but I have changed several times since then. I don't keep the same size for ten minutes together."

"What size do you want to be?" it asked.

"Well, I should like to be a little larger," said Alice. "Eight centimetres is such a wretched height to be."

"It's a very good height indeed!" said the Caterpillar angrily, rearing up. (It was exactly eight centimetres high.)

Then it got down off the mushroom and crawled away, remarking as it went, "One side of the mushroom will make you grow taller, and the other side will make you grow shorter."

Alice broke off a piece of mushroom from each side and nibbled a little of the right-hand side. The next moment her chin had struck her foot! She at once nibbled some of the other side. But alas! All of a sudden her neck was immensely long, like a snake! So she carefully nibbled first a piece from one side of the mushroom and then a piece from the other until she was her usual height. And then, seeing a little house ahead of her, she nibbled some more mushroom until she had brought herself down to twenty centimetres high and was the right size to meet the owners.

# ALICE IN WONDERLAND

As Alice approached the house, a messenger came running out of the wood and knocked loudly at the door. Then he handed a letter, nearly as large as himself, to a servant, saying in a solemn tone, "For the Duchess. An invitation from the Queen to play croquet."

There was the most extraordinary noise going on inside the house – a constant howling and sneezing, and, every now and then, a great crash, as if a dish had been broken to pieces. But Alice was intent on going inside, so she slipped past the servant and stepped through the door.

She found herself in a large kitchen. The Duchess was sitting in the middle holding a baby, and a cook was stirring a large cauldron of soup over the fire. The air was full of pepper, which made Alice, the Duchess and the baby sneeze (when the baby wasn't howling). The only things in the kitchen that were not sneezing were the cook and a large cat that was sitting on the hearth and grinning from ear to ear.

"Why does your cat grin like that?" Alice asked the Duchess timidly.

"It's a Cheshire Cat," snapped the Duchess, "and that's why."

Suddenly the cook began throwing everything within her reach at the Duchess and the baby: a large ladle, then a shower of saucepans, plates and dishes. The Duchess took no notice, even when they hit her, and the baby was howling so much already that it was quite impossible to say whether the blows hurt it or not.

# ALICE IN WONDERLAND

"Here! You may hold it a bit, if you like!" the Duchess said to Alice, flinging the baby at her. "I must get ready to play croquet with the Queen." And with that, she departed. The baby snorted and grunted in the most alarming way and, looking at it more closely, Alice saw that it was in fact a small pig. It would be quite absurd for her to hold it any longer, she thought, so she set the little creature down and watched it trot away into the wood.

Once outside the house, Alice was a little startled to see the Cheshire Cat sitting on the bough of a tree. The Cat grinned when it saw Alice. It looked good-natured, she thought, but she still felt that it ought to be treated with respect.

"Cheshire Cat," she began. "Would you tell me, please, which way I ought to go from here?"

"That depends a lot on where you want to get to," said the Cat.

Alice felt that this could not be denied, so she tried another question. "What sort of people live about here?"

"In that direction," the Cat said, waving its right paw, "lives a Hatter. And in that direction," – it waved the other paw – "lives a March Hare. Visit either you like. They're both mad."

"But I'm not sure I want to go among mad people," Alice remarked.

"Oh, you can't help that," said the Cat. "We're all mad here. Do you play croquet with the Queen today?"

"I should like to play very much," said Alice, "but I haven't been invited yet."

Suddenly, the Cat vanished.

Alice was not much surprised at this, as she was getting so used to odd things happening. She waited a little, half expecting to see the Cat again, but it did not appear, so she walked on in the direction that the March Hare was said to live.

"I've seen hatters before," she thought, "so the March Hare should be much more interesting."

As she said this, she looked up, and there was the Cat on the branch again. After a moment, the Cat vanished again, but quite slowly, beginning with the end of its tail and ending with its grin, which remained some time after the rest of it had gone.

Alice walked a little way further and then came in sight of the March Hare's house. At least, she thought it was his house, because the chimneys were shaped like ears and the roof was thatched with fur.

# ALICE IN WONDERLAND

There was a table set out under a tree, and the March Hare and the Hatter were having tea at it. A Dormouse was sitting between them, fast asleep, and the other two were talking over its head. The table was a large one, but the three were all crowded together at one corner of it.

"No room! No room!" they cried out when Alice approached.

"There's plenty of room!" said Alice indignantly, and she sat down in a large armchair at one end of the table.

"Why is a raven like a writing desk?" asked the Hatter.

Alice sat silently for a minute while she pondered the riddle. She thought over all she could remember about ravens and writing desks, which wasn't much.

"I give up," said Alice. "What's the answer?"

"I haven't the slightest idea," said the Hatter.

Alice sighed wearily. "I think you might do something better with your time than waste it asking riddles with no answers."

The Hatter shook his head mournfully. "If you knew Time as well as I do, you wouldn't talk about wasting it. Time is a him, in any case. I quarrelled with Time last March, and ever since that he won't do a thing I ask! It's always six o'clock now."

"Is that the reason so many tea things are put out here?" Alice asked.

"Yes, that's it," said the Hatter with a sigh. "It's always teatime. We've no time to wash up, so instead we have our tea, move round the table to new seats with clean dishes and have tea again." As he spoke, they all moved round.

"This is the stupidest tea party I ever was at in all my life," thought Alice. "I'll never come here again!"

And with that, she got up and walked off.

Ahead of her, Alice could see a tree with a door leading right into it. Stepping inside, she found herself back in the long hall with the little glass table, the golden key and the door to the lovely garden. She nibbled some mushroom (she had kept a piece of it in her pocket) till she was about thirty centimetres high, then walked through the door and into the garden.

In front of her was a large rose tree with white roses on it. Three gardeners were busily painting them red.

"Would you tell me," said Alice, "why you are painting those roses?"

"This ought to have been a red rose tree, miss," said one, "and we put a white one in by mistake. If the Queen were to find out, we should all have our heads cut off."

Suddenly another gardener called out, "The Queen! The Queen!" and all three gardeners instantly threw themselves flat upon their faces.

A procession approached, made up of the Knave of Hearts, a platoon of soldiers made of playing cards and the King and Queen of Hearts last of all.

When the Queen saw what the gardeners had done, she shouted "Off with their heads!" then walked away. Before the soldiers knew what was happening, Alice helped the gardeners hide in a large flowerpot nearby. After a few minutes of searching, the soldiers gave up and marched off in the direction of the Queen. Alice decided to follow them to the croquet ground.

Alice had never seen such a curious croquet ground in all her life. The balls were live hedgehogs, the mallets were live flamingos and the soldiers had to stand on all fours to make the arches. Even when Alice had succeeded in getting her flamingo's body tucked away under her arm and its neck nicely straightened out, it would twist itself round and look up in her face with a puzzled expression, which made her laugh.

And when she had got its head down to strike a hedgehog, the hedgehog unrolled itself and crawled away. It was a very difficult game indeed! Alice decided to escape without the Queen noticing.

Very soon, Alice came upon a Gryphon.

"Have you seen the Mock Turtle yet?" it asked.

"No," said Alice. "I never saw one. I don't even know what a Mock Turtle is."

"Come on then," said the Gryphon, "and he shall tell you his history."

They had not gone far before they saw the Mock Turtle, sitting sad and lonely on a little ledge of rock. As they came nearer, Alice could hear him sighing as if his heart would break.

"Why is he sad?" she asked the Gryphon.

"It's all his fancy, that," said the creature. "He's got no sorrow, you know." Then it turned to the Mock Turtle. "This here young lady wants to know your history, she do," it said.

"I'll tell it her," said the Mock Turtle.

There followed a long silence, broken only by the Mock Turtle's constant heavy sobbing.

"When we were little," it said at last, more calmly, "we went to school in the sea. The master was an old Turtle. We used to call him Tortoise."

"Why did you call him Tortoise, if he wasn't one?" Alice asked.

"We called him Tortoise because he taught us," said the Mock Turtle angrily. "Really you are very stupid!"

"And how many hours a day did you do lessons?" said Alice.

"Ten hours the first day," said the Mock Turtle, "nine the next, and so on."

"What a curious plan!" exclaimed Alice.

"That's the reason they're called lessons," the Gryphon remarked, "because they lessen from day to day."

All at once, a cry of "The trial's beginning!" was heard in the distance.

"What trial is it?" asked Alice, but the Gryphon only answered, "Come on!" Then he took her by the hand and ran.

# ALICE IN WONDERLAND

The King and Queen of Hearts were seated on their thrones when Alice arrived, with a great crowd around them – all sorts of little birds and beasts as well as the whole pack of cards. The Knave was standing in front of them in chains, and nearby was the White Rabbit, holding a trumpet and a scroll of parchment. The King was the judge, wearing a wig under his crown, and there were twelve jurors in a jury box, who were a mixture of animals and birds. In the very middle of the court was a table with tarts upon it.

"Silence in the court!" the White Rabbit cried out.

"Herald, read the accusation!" said the King.

The Rabbit blew three blasts on the trumpet, unrolled the parchment scroll and read as follows:

> "The Queen of Hearts, she made some tarts,
>
> All on a summer day.
>
> The Knave of Hearts, he stole those tarts,
>
> And took them clean away!"

"Consider your verdict," the King said to the jury.

"Not yet, not yet!" the Rabbit hastily interrupted. "There's a lot to come before that!"

"Call the first witness," said the King, and the White Rabbit called out, "The Hatter!"

The Mad Hatter came in with a teacup in one hand and a piece of bread and butter in the other.

"I beg pardon, your Majesty, but I hadn't quite finished my tea when I was sent for."

"Give your evidence," said the King, "and don't be nervous, or I'll have you executed on the spot."

Just at this moment Alice felt a very curious sensation: she was beginning to grow larger again.

"I'm a poor man, your Majesty," said the Hatter miserably.

"You're a very poor speaker," said the King. "You may go. Call the next witness!"

Alice leapt up in surprise when the White Rabbit read out, "Alice!"

"Here I am!" cried Alice. She jumped up in a hurry, quite forgetting how large she had grown in the last few minutes, and tipped over the jury box with the edge of her skirt. The jurors flew out.

"Oh, I beg your pardon," she exclaimed.

When the jurors were back in their seats, the King said to Alice, "What do you know about this business?"

"Nothing," said Alice.

"Nothing whatever?" persisted the King.

"Nothing whatever," said Alice.

Then the King read out from a book, "Rule forty-two. All persons more than a mile high to leave the court."

Everybody looked at Alice.

"I'm not a mile high," said Alice.

"You are," said the King.

"Nearly two miles high," added the Queen.

"Well, I shan't go, at any rate," said Alice. "You invented that rule just now."

The King turned pale. "Consider your verdict," he said to the jury.

"No, no!" said the Queen. "Sentence first, verdict afterwards."

"Stuff and nonsense!" said Alice loudly. "The idea of having the sentence first!"

"Hold your tongue!" said the Queen, turning purple.

"I won't!" said Alice.

"Off with her head!" the Queen shouted at the top of her voice.

"Who cares for you?" said Alice (who had grown to her full size by this time). "You're nothing but a pack of cards!"

At this, the whole pack rose up into the air and came flying down upon her. She gave a little scream and tried to beat them off. The next moment she found herself lying on the bank with her head in the lap of her sister, who was gently brushing away some dead leaves that had fluttered down from the trees upon her face.

"Wake up, Alice dear!" said her sister. "What a long sleep you've had!"

"I've had such a curious dream!" said Alice, and she told her sister all her strange adventures. Then she ran off home for tea, thinking while she ran, as well she might, what a wonderful dream it had been.

# THE WIND IN THE WILLOWS

The Mole had been working very hard all the morning spring cleaning his little home. Spring was moving in the air, filling even his dark and lowly little house with longing. It was small wonder, then, that suddenly he could bear it no longer. He scraped and scratched and scrabbled and scrooged, working busily with his little paws till at last, pop! His snout came out into the sunlight.

He rambled happily across the meadow until he came to the river. Never in his life had he seen a river before – a sleek, sinuous, full-bodied animal, chasing and chuckling. The Mole was bewitched.

In the bank opposite he noticed a dark hole. As he watched, one eye then another appeared, in a small brown face with whiskers, neat ears and thick, silky hair. It was the Water Rat.

"Would you like to come over?" asked the Rat.

He stepped into a little boat and rowed smartly across before helping the Mole to step gingerly on board.

"Believe me," said the Rat, "there is nothing half so much worth doing as simply messing about in boats."

They rowed gently on for a while, but soon Mole was so excited by the light, the sound and the smell of the river that he cried out, "Ratty! Please, I want to row, now!"

And though the Rat tried to stop him, the Mole jumped up to seize the oars, the boat tipped and – sploosh! Both animals were in the water.

Poor Mole! Rat helped him to the bank while he coughed and spluttered, feeling thoroughly ashamed of himself. But when Mole started to apologize, Rat laughed. "What's a little wet to a water rat? Why don't you come and stay with me for a little time? I can teach you to row and to swim, and you'll soon be as handy on the water as any of us!"

So Mole went to stay in Rat's comfortable waterside home.

"Ratty," said the Mole suddenly, one bright morning, "if you please, won't you take me to call on Mr Toad? I've heard so much about him, and I do so want to make his acquaintance."

"Why, certainly," said the good-natured Rat. "Get the boat out, and we'll paddle up there at once. It's never the wrong time to call on Toad. Always good-tempered, always glad to see you, always sorry when you go, he is!"

"He must be a very nice animal," observed the Mole, as he got into the boat and started to row.

"He is indeed the best of animals," replied the Rat. "He does have his crazes, though. Once, it was nothing but sailing. He bought sailing boats, sailing clothes, sailing everything! Then he tired of that and took to houseboating, and we all had to stay with him in his houseboat and pretend we liked it. He was going to spend the rest of his life in a houseboat. It's always the same, whatever he takes up. He gets tired of it and starts on something fresh."

Rounding a bend in the river, they came in sight of Toad Hall, a handsome old house with lawns reaching down to the water's edge. They disembarked, strolled up to the house and found Toad resting in a garden chair.

"Hooray!" Toad cried upon seeing them. "I was just about to send a boat to fetch you. I've discovered what I want to do for the rest of my life."

Rat sighed and looked knowingly at Mole.

Toad led them to the stable yard, where he pointed to a gypsy caravan painted a canary yellow with green and red wheels. A horse was already harnessed to it. "That's the only way to travel!" cried Toad. "The open road, the dusty highway, the rolling hills! Here today, up and off to somewhere else tomorrow! All complete inside with everything we'll need when we make our start this afternoon."

Rat needed to be persuaded to leave his beloved river for another of Toad's crazes, but later that afternoon, the three friends set off.

It was a golden afternoon. The friends spent several hours rambling happily along narrow lanes in Toad's caravan.

It was not till much later that they came out on the high road. They were now strolling along easily, chatting together happily, when far behind them they heard a faint hum, like the drone of a distant bee. A faint 'Poop-poop!' wailed like an uneasy animal in pain. Glancing back, Toad and Rat saw a cloud of dust with a dark centre of energy. It was advancing on them at incredible speed, but, not knowing what it was, they simply carried on their conversation.

In an instant, the peaceful scene was changed. With a blast of wind and a whirl of sound, 'Poop-poop!' rang in their ears, and a magnificent motor car, immense and breathtaking, with its driver tense and hugging the wheel, roared down upon them, flung a cloud of dust around them, then dwindled to a speck in the far distance.

The horse, who had been dreaming of his quiet paddock, suddenly reared, plunged and, though Mole tried to stop him, drove the caravan backwards into the deep ditch by the side of the road. It wavered an instant; there was a heart-wrenching crash – and the canary-coloured caravan, their pride and joy, lay on its side, a total wreck.

Rat hopped up and down, shaking his fists, while the Mole tried to quiet the horse. Toad, however, sat in the middle of the dusty road and stared after the disappearing motor car, faintly murmuring, "Poop-poop!"

"Now that's the only way to travel!" he sighed. "Freedom to go wherever you want, as fast as you want!"

"What are we to do with him?" asked Mole.

"Nothing at all," replied the Rat. "He has got a new craze and will be quite useless for all practical purposes."

They carried Toad to the nearest town, arranged for the caravan and horse to be picked up and took the first train home.

# THE WIND IN THE WILLOWS

After their adventure with Toad, life for the Mole and the Rat settled back into its peaceful ways again. But then Mole asked to meet another of Rat's friends, Mr Badger, who lived in the middle of the deep, dark Wild Wood.

"Badger's a shy animal and doesn't leave the Wild Wood often. He'll turn up some day or other, and I'll introduce you," said the Rat. But the Badger never turned up, and late one December afternoon, while the Rat dozed, the Mole decided to go and find him.

When he first stepped into the Wild Wood, twigs crackled under his feet and logs tripped him, but that was all fun and exciting. But then the faces began to appear: little, evil, wedge-shaped faces, looking at him. Then the whistling began: very faint and shrill, far behind him, then far ahead of him. And then the pattering began: the patter of little feet. The whole wood seemed to be hunting now, closing in around the Mole. He began to run, until eventually, exhausted and terrified, he took refuge in a hollow.

When Rat woke up, he realized that Mole was not at home. Fresh tracks outside led directly to the Wild Wood, and Rat was worried: the Wild Wood animals could be dangerous. He put on his coat and set off to find his friend.

After an hour's searching, Rat found
Mole, huddled in the hollow. The light had
nearly gone, and Rat was keen to start for home,
but Mole was too weak and scared to move. By the
time Rat had comforted him and urged him to begin
the journey back, there was thick snow on the ground.
The wood looked completely different. The friends
struggled on for an hour or two, but they became
hopelessly lost. Then the Mole tripped on something
under the snow and stumbled.

"What was that?" said the Rat, looking at the
ground. He dug in the snow and uncovered a metal
scraper for cleaning boots. After further digging in the
snow bank, Rat found a door with a bell-pull and a brass
plate engraved with the words 'Mr Badger'.

# THE WIND IN THE WILLOWS

Rat and Mole rapped on the door until it opened to reveal a long snout and a pair of small, blinking eyes.

"Ratty, my dear man!" exclaimed the Badger on seeing his friend. "Come in, both of you! Out in the snow and in the Wild Wood, too!"

The two animals tumbled over each other in their eagerness to get inside, where Badger offered them a large, warm kitchen, a roaring fire, dressing gowns, slippers and safety.

# THE WIND IN THE WILLOWS

When they had eaten dinner, Rat and Mole told Badger about their evening's adventures. Badger nodded gravely. Then he asked them about Toad.

"The rumour on the river is that he's going from bad to worse," said the Rat. "He's had seven cars and seven smashes, been in hospital three times and, as for the speeding fines he's had to pay…"

Badger thought hard. "I can't do anything in the winter," he said, "but in the spring, we – that is, you and me and our friend the Mole here – we'll take Toad seriously in hand. We'll make him a sensible Toad, by force if need be."

Rat and Mole slept soundly that night. Mole felt so at home in Badger's comfortable burrow – it reminded him of his own underground home – and he told Badger so.

"Once underground," Mole said, "nothing can happen to you, and nothing can get at you. Things go on overhead, and, when you want to, up you go, and there they are, waiting for you."

The Badger simply beamed at him. "That's exactly what I say," he replied. "By the way," he said confidentially, "I'll pass the word around the Wild Wood, and you'll have no further trouble from the inhabitants. They're not so bad, really. And anyway, any friend of mine walks where he likes!"

By this time, Rat was eager to get back to his river. So goodbyes were said, and Badger took the friends through underground tunnels to the very edge of the wood. Then they set off for home, firelight, familiar things and the beloved river.

Mole and Rat did not see Badger again until early the next summer, but when he turned up, he had Toad on his mind.

"I have heard," he said sternly, "that Toad is to have a new and exceptionally powerful motor car delivered today. You must come with me instantly and save him from himself."

When the friends got to Toad Hall, a shiny new motor car stood outside, and Toad, dressed in goggles, cap and enormous gloves, was looking very pleased with himself. When Badger suggested that he should give up motor cars for good, Toad refused with great spirit. Badger then turned to the chauffeur in charge of the car and said, "I'm afraid that Mr Toad has changed his mind. He does not want to buy the car."

The chauffeur drove it away, and Rat and Mole hustled the protesting Toad into his bedroom and locked the door. There he stayed, under lock and key, guarded day and night, for several weeks. It was the only way to stop Toad buying another car and getting into trouble.

As time passed, Toad's car madness appeared to be under control. But, in fact, he was planning his escape. One day, when his captors were otherwise occupied, he dressed himself in a smart suit, filled his pockets with cash and escaped out of his bedroom window, feeling pleased with himself.

Toad was about halfway through lunch at a local inn when he heard a car turn into the yard. He had not seen or driven a car for weeks, and he couldn't stop himself. The next moment he had stolen it and was sitting in the driver's seat, revving the engine and speeding through the open country! He sped he knew not where, not caring what might happen to him.

When he was caught, Toad was arrested and charged with stealing and with driving dangerously. He was also rude to the police, which didn't help his case. The judge sentenced him to twenty years in prison.

# THE WIND IN THE WILLOWS

Toad flung himself on the floor of his cell in despair. "This is the end of everything," he said. "At least it is the end of Toad, which is the same thing." Day after day, he cried and howled, and refused to eat or drink.

Then, one day, the gaoler's daughter, who was very fond of animals, knocked on the door of his cell. "Cheer up, Toad," she said. "I've brought you some tea and toast." Toad sat up and saw the toast, dripping with golden butter. He took a bite and a sip of tea while the girl asked him about himself. Soon he felt much better.

Over the following weeks, the girl began to feel sorry for Toad. One morning, she said, "Toad, I have an aunt who does the washing for all the prisoners here. She takes it out on Monday and brings it in again on Friday. Today is Thursday. I believe I could disguise you in her dress and bonnet tomorrow, and you could escape. You're very alike in many respects – particularly about the figure."

"We're not," said the Toad in a huff. "I have a very elegant figure."

"So has my aunt!" replied the girl.

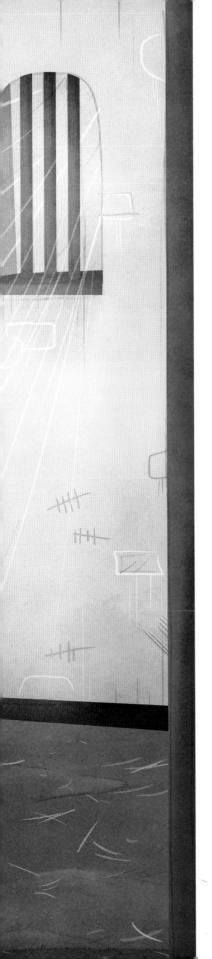

Though Toad thought it beneath him to dress as a washerwoman, this was a great opportunity, so he agreed to the plan.

The next evening, the girl ushered her aunt into Toad's cell. The girl helped Toad put on a cotton gown, an apron, a shawl and a black bonnet.

"Goodbye, Toad," she said, "and good luck!"

With a quaking heart, Toad set forth on what he thought would be a most hazardous adventure. But, to his surprise, everything was remarkably easy. The washerwoman's outfit seemed to be a passport for every barred door and gate. At last he heard the great outer door click behind him and knew that he was free!

Toad walked quickly towards the nearest railway station, but, when he went to buy his ticket, he realized that he had left his coat in the cell, and all his money with it. Full of despair, with tears trickling down each side of his nose, he wandered down the platform to where a train was standing.

"Hullo, ma'am!" said the engine driver. "What's the trouble?"

"Oh, sir!" said Toad. "I've lost all my money and can't pay for a ticket, and I must get home tonight somehow."

"Well, I'll tell you what I'll do," said the driver. "If you'll wash a few shirts for me when you get home, and send 'em along, I'll give you a ride on my engine."

Toad scrambled up into the cab. The train moved out of the station and its speed increased, every moment taking Toad nearer to Toad Hall. But, after some time, another engine appeared on the rails behind them, crowded with policemen waving and shouting, "Stop, stop, stop!"

"Save me, dear kind Mr Engine Driver!" pleaded Toad. "I am not the simple washerwoman I seem to be! I am a toad – the well-known and popular Mr Toad – just escaped from a loathsome prison." When the engine driver listened to Toad's crimes he said, "You have indeed been a wicked Toad. But the sight of an animal in tears makes me feel soft-hearted. So cheer up! We may beat them yet!"

They piled on more coal to speed up, but still their pursuers gained on them.

"There's one thing left," said the driver, "and it's your only chance. There's a long tunnel ahead and thick woods on the other side. When we are through, I will put on the brakes, and you must jump out and hide. Then I will go full speed again, and they can chase me if they like."

When the driver gave the word, Toad
jumped, rolled down a hill, scrambled into the
wood and hid. Out of the tunnel burst the
other train, but Toad fled further into
the wood, leaving the railway as
far behind as possible.

Toad found a safe spot in the wood and fell asleep. He awoke the following morning in bright sunlight. He marched forth, cold but confident, hungry but hopeful, along a rustic road, which was soon joined by a canal. A long, low barge boat soon came along the water. On the deck stood a strong-looking woman.

"A nice morning, ma'am!" she remarked to Toad.

"I daresay it is, ma'am," said Toad politely, "but I've lost all my money and my way! I need to get to Toad Hall."

"Why, I'm going that way myself," replied the barge woman. "I'll give you a lift."

"You're in the washing business, aren't you, ma'am?" said the woman thoughtfully, as Toad stepped lightly on board. "There's a heap of my clothes in the corner of the cabin. If you'll just take one or two and wash them as we go along, why, it'll be a real help to me."

Toad was worried. He fetched the washtub and soap, selected a few pieces of clothing and started to wash. A long half hour passed, and every minute of it saw Toad getting crosser and crosser. Nothing he could do to the clothes seemed to get them clean.

The barge woman started to laugh at him. "You've never washed so much as a shirt in your life!"

"I would have you know that I am a very well-known, distinguished Toad, and I will not be laughed at by anyone!" said Toad in fury.

"Why, so you are!" cried the woman, moving nearer. "A horrid, nasty, crawly Toad! And in my nice clean barge too!"

She caught him by one front leg and one hind leg, and suddenly Toad found himself flying through the air.

He landed in cold, deep water that swept him swiftly along into a river. There was a big, dark hole in the bank above his head, so he caught hold of the edge and held on. Something was inching towards him in the hole. A face gradually became clear and familiar. Brown and small, with whiskers... it was Rat!

Rat gripped Toad firmly and pulled him inside his home. Then he sent Toad upstairs to wash and put on fresh clothes. "Never in my whole life have I seen a shabbier, more disreputable object than you, Toad!" he cried.

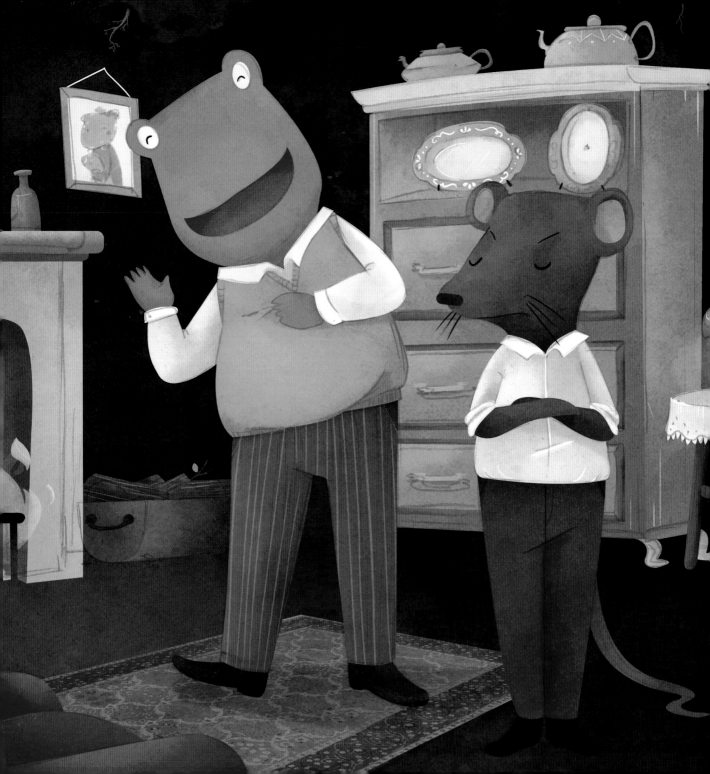

When he had changed, Toad started to tell all his adventures, dwelling mainly on his own cleverness. But the more he talked and boasted, the more silent Rat became.

"I don't want to give you pain, Toady," said Rat, "but do you mean that you've heard nothing about the ferrets and stoats and weasels and how they've taken over Toad Hall?"

"No! Not a word!" cried Toad, trembling in every limb.

"When you got into trouble, the Wild Wood animals said that you would never come back. One night they moved into Toad Hall and declared they were there for good. They've got guards all around, and they're all armed. Mole and Badger have been watching them and planning how to get your house back."

There was a knock at the door. It was Mr Badger, closely followed by the Mole. They were both shabby and unwashed but greeted Toad warmly. Then they described the situation up at Toad Hall.

"The ferrets and stoats and weasels make the best guards in the world," said Badger solemnly. "But I've got a great secret: there's an underground passage that leads from the riverbank into the middle of Toad Hall. There's going to be a big party at the Hall tomorrow night – it's the Chief Weasel's birthday, I believe – and all the weasels will be gathered in the dining room, eating and drinking with no weapons to hand. The guards will be posted as usual, but the passage leads right up next to the dining room, so we don't need to worry about them."

"So we shall creep in quietly," cried the Mole.

"With our swords and sticks!" shouted the Rat.

"And rush in upon them!" said the Badger.

"And give them the fright of their lives!" cried the Toad.

Toad went off to bed, thinking that he was too excited to sleep. But the sheets and blankets were very friendly and comforting, after having slept on plain straw on a stone floor in a draughty cell, and he soon began to snore happily.

He awoke late the next morning to find that the other animals had finished breakfast some time ago. Rat was running round the room busily, with his arms full of equipment of every kind. He was distributing them in four little heaps on the floor, saying excitedly under his breath, "Here's-a-stick-for-the-Rat, here's-a-stick-for-the-Mole, here's-a-stick-for-the-Toad, here's-a-stick-for-the-Badger! Here's-a-rope-for-the-Rat…" and so on, while the four little heaps gradually grew and grew.

When it began to get dark, the Badger took a lantern in one paw, grasped his stick with the other and led the others into the secret passage. They shuffled along until the Badger sensed that they were nearly under the dining room at Toad Hall. Such a tremendous noise of stamping feet and shouts of laughter was going on above that there was little danger of being heard. They hurried along till they were standing under a trapdoor.

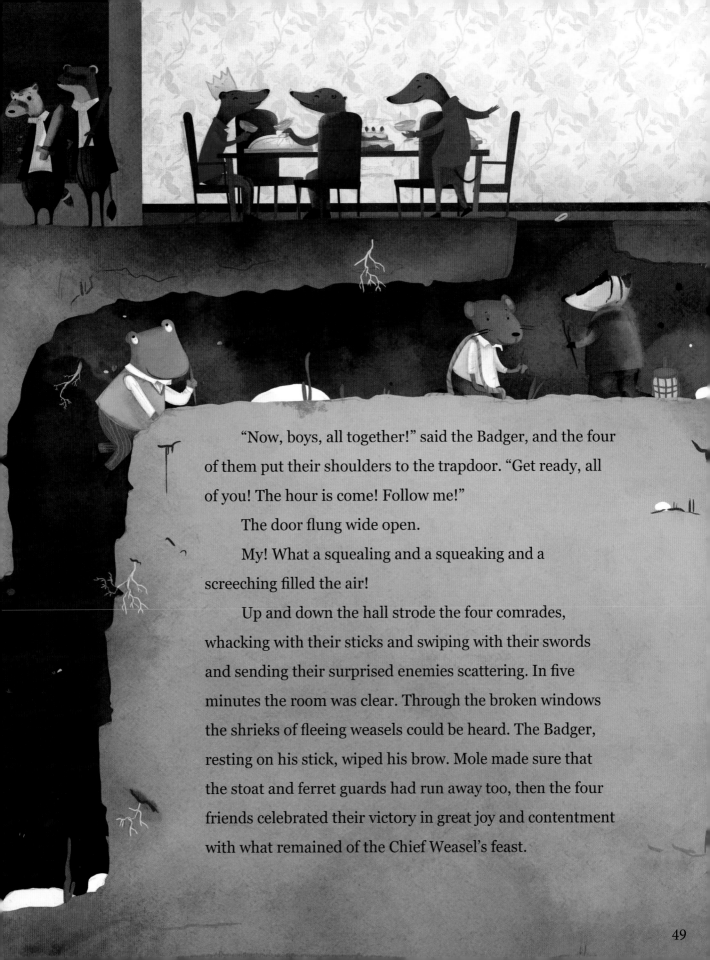

"Now, boys, all together!" said the Badger, and the four of them put their shoulders to the trapdoor. "Get ready, all of you! The hour is come! Follow me!"

The door flung wide open.

My! What a squealing and a squeaking and a screeching filled the air!

Up and down the hall strode the four comrades, whacking with their sticks and swiping with their swords and sending their surprised enemies scattering. In five minutes the room was clear. Through the broken windows the shrieks of fleeing weasels could be heard. The Badger, resting on his stick, wiped his brow. Mole made sure that the stoat and ferret guards had run away too, then the four friends celebrated their victory in great joy and contentment with what remained of the Chief Weasel's feast.

The following morning, all the animals agreed to have a banquet to celebrate their victory in the Battle of Toad Hall. Toad's job was to write the invitations. "You must do it," said Badger. "You own Toad Hall, after all, so you're the host."

Toad didn't want to write boring letters when he could be swaggering around the Hall enjoying himself! But then he had an idea: he would write them and mention his leading part in the fight and how he defeated the Chief Weasel, and he would hint at his adventures and triumphs!

Badger was suspicious about Toad's change of heart, so when the invitations were ready for posting, Rat opened and read a couple.

"They're disgraceful!" he told Badger. "Full of pride and swagger. Toad doesn't realize that he has done anything wrong in his life!" So Mole rewrote the invitations, and Badger and Rat solemnly took Toad aside and told him how bad he had been.

At last the banquet arrived. All the guests cheered Toad and congratulated him on his courage, his cleverness and his fighting qualities. But Toad only smiled faintly and murmured, "Not at all! Badger was the mastermind; the Mole and Water Rat bore the brunt of the fighting; I did very little."

The animals were puzzled by his modesty, and, much to Toad's surprise, he realized that he didn't need to brag to be the centre of attention. Badger and Rat stared at him open-mouthed, giving him the greatest satisfaction of all.

In fact, Toad became such a reformed character that the police dropped the charges against him. Though life became peaceful again, the brave actions of the four friends were not forgotten. Sometimes they would stroll through the Wild Wood, now successfully tamed. As they passed, mother weasels would say to their young ones, "Look, baby! There goes the great Mr Toad, the gallant Water Rat, the famous Mr Mole and, next to him, the fearsome Mr Badger!"

Of course, the friends were not fearsome warriors at all, but it made them chuckle to think that they might be considered so.

# TREASURE ISLAND

Squire Trelawney and Dr Livesey have asked me to write down all the details about Treasure Island, from beginning to end, keeping nothing back but the whereabouts of the island, and that only because there may still be treasure to be found. I take up my pen and go back to the time when my parents kept the Admiral Benbow inn and the old seaman with the sabre cut across his cheek first took up his lodging under our roof.

I remember him as if it were yesterday, glancing about suspiciously and whistling to himself, and then breaking out in that old sea-song that he sang so often, "Fifteen men on the dead man's chest, yo-ho-ho, and a bottle of rum!"

"Much company here, mate?" he growled at my father, as he plodded up to our door, dragging a large chest behind him. My father shook his head.

"Then this is the place for me," he snarled. "Name's Billy Bones, but you can call me Captain."

He beckoned to me with his dirty, scarred hands. "Boy, if you keep an eye open for a seafaring man with one leg, I'll pay you a silver penny the first of every month."

I loved a mystery and promised him I would do his bidding.

The strange seaman stayed for months, but he never paid my parents a penny for his keep. Every day he strolled along the cove cliffs, looking out to sea with a telescope; every evening he sat in the parlour drinking rum.

It was during the Captain's stay that my father became ill and passed away. Two mysterious events also occurred around this sad time, which rid us of the Captain.

# TREASURE ISLAND

The first happened one frosty morning, when the Captain was out on his usual cliff walk. A pale man, missing two fingers on his left hand and carrying a cutlass, came into the inn, sat down and demanded a drink.

As he was asking me whether we had a captain staying with us, Billy Bones strode through the door.

"Hello, Bill," said the man. "You remember your ol' shipmate?"

The Captain gave a sort of gasp. "Black Dog!" he cried.

"And who else?" cackled the man.

"What do yer want?" whispered the Captain.

"I've come for what you've hidden in your sea chest," sneered Black Dog. "Hand it over, and there'll be no trouble."

"Never!" roared the Captain, and he pulled out his own cutlass.

There followed a terrible sword fight and then a cry of pain, and, in the next instant, I saw Black Dog fleeing from the inn with blood streaming from his shoulder.

# TREASURE ISLAND

The Captain's face had turned a horrible colour. "I've got to get away from here. Jim, help me. Black Dog and me sailed with a pirate named Captain Flint. I was his first mate, and he gave me for safe-keeping a map of where he buried his treasure. The rest of his crew will be after me now, for sure." And with these words, he reeled a little, caught himself with one hand against the wall and then fell with a heavy thud to the floor.

According to our good friend Dr Livesey, he'd had a stroke. Whether it was from too much rum or from shock, I'll never know.

While the Captain was recovering in bed, the second mysterious event occurred. I was outside the inn when I heard an odd tapping noise. I turned to see an old blind man trudging up the road towards me.

"Can any kind friend tell me where I am?" he cried.

"You are at the Admiral Benbow inn," I called out.

Suddenly, the man grabbed my arm and hissed in a cruel, cold voice, "Take me in to the Captain."

Terrified, I obeyed him. The sickly Captain paled even more when he saw the old man.

"Hold out your hand, Bill," growled the blind man, and he pressed a small piece of paper into the Captain's hand. He turned and, tapping his stick, left as suddenly as he had appeared.

Bill read the note on the back. "The Black Spot! The pirates, they're coming for me at ten o'clock tonight!" he gasped, as he leapt out of bed. In the next moment, with a peculiar sound, he fell to the floor. To my horror and great distress, he was dead.

With the Captain's last words weighing heavy on my heart, I ran to my mother and lost no time in telling her all that I knew and perhaps should have told her long before. We realized we were now in a difficult and dangerous position. With little time to lose, we made our plans. We would have to leave the inn before the pirates arrived. We decided we would seek shelter and help from Dr Livesey.

Before we left, my mother told me to search the Captain's dead body for the key to his sea chest. She was convinced there would be money in the chest, and some of the Captain's money – if indeed there was any – was certainly due to us for his stay at the inn. She said we should take what was owed to us, because it was not likely that our Captain's old shipmates, who would certainly be here before long, would be inclined to give up their booty in payment of the dead man's debts.

Overcoming my disgust at having to touch the dead Captain, I tore open his shirt at the neck and there, hanging on a bit of dirty string, I found the key. We ran to the chest and unlocked it.

A strong smell of tobacco and tar rose from the interior. Underneath some clothes and an odd assortment of trinkets and shells, we found a bundle of papers tied up in oilcloth and a bag filled with coins from many countries. We grabbed the papers and some of the coins and crept out into the foggy night not a moment too soon. The sound of running footsteps came to our ears, and, as we looked back, we could see the light of a lantern bobbing in the dark, heading towards our inn.

"My dear," said my mother suddenly, "take the money and run on. I am going to faint." And she crumpled to the ground.

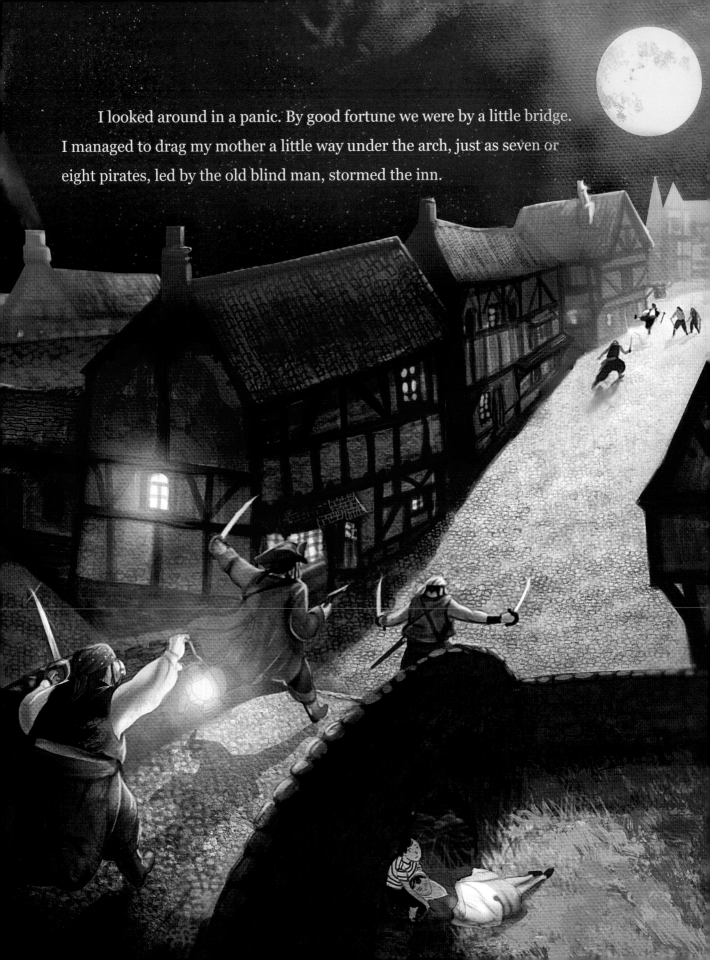

I looked around in a panic. By good fortune we were by a little bridge.
I managed to drag my mother a little way under the arch, just as seven or
eight pirates, led by the old blind man, stormed the inn.

I could hear the fury in the blind man's voice as he cried, "Is Flint's map there?"

"The money's here, but I don't see no map," replied one of the men.

"It's that boy and his mother. They must have it! Scatter, lads, and find 'em."

I lay by the bridge and watched in horror as the pirates tore apart the inn in their desperate search. Suddenly, a sharp whistle pierced the night.

"We'll have to budge, mates. There's trouble on the way!" cried one of the men.

"You've got to find the map," screamed the blind man. "We'll be as rich as kings if you find it!"

But the other pirates, fearing for their own safety, grabbed the money and started running in all directions, as the sound of galloping hooves came thundering down the road.

Screaming and cursing, the blind man staggered along the road, tapping his stick in a frenzy, and, before I knew it, he had stumbled into the path of the galloping horses. The riders couldn't stop in time, and, to my horror, the blind man was trampled to death under the hooves.

I leaped to my feet and hailed the riders. They were revenue officers who had heard some news about the pirates' intended raid and had been on their way to stop them. I hurriedly told them my story and about my fear that the pirates would be back for the bundle of papers I had taken from the Captain's chest.

After helping my mother to the village to recover from her faint, the supervising officer agreed to take me to see Dr Livesey to give him the papers for safe-keeping.

Dr Livesey was dining with the squire, Mr Trelawney, when I arrived. The two men listened to my story with surprise and interest.

"You've heard of this Flint, I suppose?" said the doctor to the squire.

"Heard of him?" cried the squire. "He was the blood-thirstiest buccaneer that ever sailed!"

The doctor carefully opened the seals on one of the papers, revealing a map of an island, with three red crosses marked on it. By the last cross, written in a small neat hand, were the words, 'Bulk of treasure here'.

*Bulk of treasure here*

# TREASURE ISLAND

The squire picked up the map, his hand shaking with excitement.

There were more scribbles on the back of it. I didn't understand the meaning of these words, but they filled the squire and Dr Livesey with delight.

"Livesey," said the squire, "we shall find this treasure! Tomorrow I will go to the port at Bristol, and in three weeks' time I'll have the best ship, sir, and the choicest crew in England."

He turned to me. "Jim Hawkins, you'll make a famous cabin boy. You, Livesey, will be ship's doctor, and I'm admiral. We'll take some men with us that I know and trust, and we'll recruit the rest of the crew."

"All right," said the excited doctor. "I'll sail with you. But none of us must breathe a word about this map."

The weeks passed slowly, for I was eager to start our treasure hunt. Finally, one fine day, Dr Livesey and I received a letter from Mr Trelawney requesting that we join him in Bristol, ready for our adventure to Treasure Island. We would be sailing on the *Hispaniola*, the ship he had bought and fitted out. He had also got a crew together, complete with ship's cook, mate and captain.

"Dear Livesey..." he wrote, "by a stroke of good fortune, I fell in talk with an old sailor who wanted a good berth as a ship's cook. Long John Silver he is called, and he has lost a leg. Out of pure pity for his state of health, I employed him on the spot. He keeps a public house here and knows all the seafaring men in Bristol. Between Silver and myself, we have got together a crew of the toughest old salts imaginable – not pretty to look at, but fellows, by their faces, of the strongest spirit. Come full speed to Bristol. John Trelawney."

I said goodbye to my mother and at last set off to Bristol. The doctor had gone the night before, and he and the squire were waiting for me at a large inn.

"Bravo! Here you are," cried the squire excitedly. "The ship's company is complete. We sail tomorrow! Come, you must meet Silver and Captain Smollett before we sail."

Now to tell you the truth, from the first mention of Long John Silver, I had taken a fear in my mind that he might prove to be the very one-legged sailor whom I had watched for at the Admiral Benbow. But one look at this clean and pleasant-tempered man was enough for me to be convinced that he was no buccaneer, and I immediately warmed to the strange old fellow.

I even warmed to his parrot, who would sit on his shoulder and say repeatedly, "Pieces of eight! Pieces of eight!" Long John told me stories of her adventures and spoke of her fondly, making me think he was the very best of men.

Smollett was a different kettle of fish altogether. He was sharp-looking and seemed angry with everything and everyone on board. He was soon to tell myself, Trelawney and Livesey why.

"Well, sir," he addressed the squire, "better to speak plain, I believe, even at the risk of offence. I don't like this cruise, and I don't like the men. That's the short and sweet."

The squire was angry to hear this, but the doctor asked Smollett to explain himself some more.

"I don't like that all the men on board seem to know more about the plans for this journey than I do, like the fact that I have only just found out that we are going after treasure. Too many people know about this treasure, and that's foolhardy." Captain Smollett sighed as he continued. "As for the men, I don't like them, sir. I think I should have had the choosing of my own hands."

"In other words, you fear a mutiny?" asked Dr Livesey.

"I wouldn't say so in so many words, but it is the captain's job to be cautious," replied Captain Smollett. "I recommend that you keep all Silver's men together, in one cabin room, away from the area on the ship where we're keeping the arms and gunpowder... just to be on the safe side."

And with that he left to organize the crew so that we could set sail on the next tide.

I am not going to relate the voyage in detail, but before we arrived at Treasure Island, something happened that I must record. Captain Smollett had been right not to trust the crew chosen by Long John Silver.

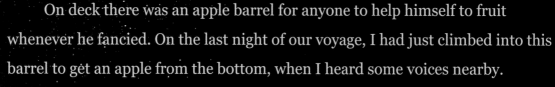

On deck there was an apple barrel for anyone to help himself to fruit whenever he fancied. On the last night of our voyage, I had just climbed into this barrel to get an apple from the bottom, when I heard some voices nearby.

"... I was Cap'n Flint's second-in-command, and I knows all about the treasure buried on this island," Silver was explaining to several of his men. "If you join me, we can all get a share of the riches. Then, as soon as we get the treasure on board, I'll finish with the Captain and his men on the island."

I was so shaken by Silver's words that I decided to stay hidden in the barrel. I realized with great fear that Silver was actually a pirate and that he was indeed planning a mutiny!

The men toasted each other with a drink of rum. "Here's to Captain Flint, and here's to us and plenty of prizes!"

Just then, as the moon rose in the night sky, the voice of the lookout shouted, "Land ahoy!"

In the following chaos, as the crew rushed on deck, I crept out of the barrel and ran to tell the Captain and the squire what I had overheard.

After listening carefully, the Captain thanked me, turned to the squire and said, "We can't let on that we know of their plans, otherwise there'll be a mutiny right now. We have time until we find the treasure. I reckon there are seven of us, including the boy and ourselves, whom we can rely on. So we must be prepared to fight these nineteen scoundrels."

The next day, with the *Hispaniola* safely anchored offshore, Captain Smollett gave orders for the men to go ashore for an afternoon off. Silver and twelve of his men eagerly got the boats ready. It was at this point that it occurred to me to slip ashore with the pirates to see what they were up to.

# TREASURE ISLAND

I hid in one of the boats, and, as soon as it reached the beach, I swung myself out and plunged into the nearest thicket. Silver saw me and started shouting my name, but I paid him no attention. Jumping and ducking, I ran until I could run no more.

I began to enjoy myself and looked around me with some interest at the strange land that I was in. I had crossed a marshy area full of odd swampy trees, and now I had come out upon the skirts of an open piece of undulating, sandy country. On the far side of this stood a hill with two craggy peaks shining vividly in the sun.

I had just reached a long thicket of oak-like trees when I heard Silver's voice. Trembling with fear, I dived for cover.

"I like you, Tom," Silver was saying. "That's why I'm asking you to join us, to save your neck."

"I'd rather lose my hand than join you scoundrels…"

Tom started to shout.

Just then a terrible scream rose through the trees.

"What was that?" cried Tom.

"Oh, I reckon that'll be Alan," grinned Silver.

"God rest his soul," murmured Tom, realizing his friend must be dead. "As for you, John Silver, you're a mate of mine no more. Kill me too, if you can."

And with that, this brave fellow turned his back on Silver and set off walking for the beach. With a cry, Silver seized a branch and hurled it at the man. It hit him with stunning violence, right between the shoulders. Tom's hands flew up, he gave a sort of gasp and he fell to the ground, dead.

I do not know what it rightly is to faint, but I do know that for the next little while the whole world swam away from before me in a whirling mist. Then, trembling, I crawled out of the thicket and ran, as fast as I could, away from the monster that was Long John Silver.

A while later, I stopped to get my bearings. It was then that I became aware of a strange figure darting among the trees ahead. What was this new danger?

Grasping my pistol, I gathered my courage and walked briskly towards the figure.

"Who are you?" I asked.

"I'm Ben Gunn," the strange man answered, his voice hoarse. His clothes were in tatters and his skin was darkened by the sun. "I was marooned three years ago. I was with Flint's crew when he buried the treasure. But he tricked me and left me stranded on the island. Please help me to escape!"

I felt sorry for Gunn, even though he had been part of Flint's pirate crew. I was starting to tell him my tale when we heard the distant boom of what sounded like a cannon being fired.

"They have begun to fight!" I cried. "Follow me, I must get back to help my friends." And we set off at a run, back towards the beach.

I found out later that Dr Livesey, Mr Trelawney, Captain Smollett and the three faithful hands had battled with the six men that Silver had left on board the *Hispaniola* and had managed to escape from the ship, taking some food supplies and arms to an old fort they had spied on shore. They had persuaded one of Silver's men, Abraham Gray, to switch sides and join them.

They were now holed up in the fort, and this was how I found them, preparing themselves for a long battle with Silver and his remaining men.

For my part, I was greatly relieved to find my friends, and they were glad to see me, as they had feared for my safety. I told them about my strange encounter with Ben Gunn and his bizarre story.

Captain Smollett gave us all jobs and divided us into watches. We collected firewood and ate a hearty meal of pork.

Throughout the night we took it in turns to guard our fort. As the sun rose on another day, we saw someone hobbling towards us. It was Long

"Who goes there? Stand down or we fire!" shouted Captain Smollett.

"Flag of truce," cried Silver. "Cap'n Silver, sir, to come and make terms."

"I have no desire to talk to you. If you wish to talk to me, you can come forward. We won't shoot," replied Smollett.

"We're willing to submit, if we can come to terms," said Silver. "We want that treasure. You have a chart, haven't you?"

"That may be, but I'll never give it to you," cried Smollett.

Silver's face went bright red. "I'll attack your ol' fort before an hour's out. You'll be wishing you'd listened to ol' Long John Silver then!" With that, he stumbled off and disappeared among the trees.

True to his word, within the hour, Silver was back with his men. A terrible battle followed. As pirates swarmed over the fort's walls, swords clashed and screams pierced the air.

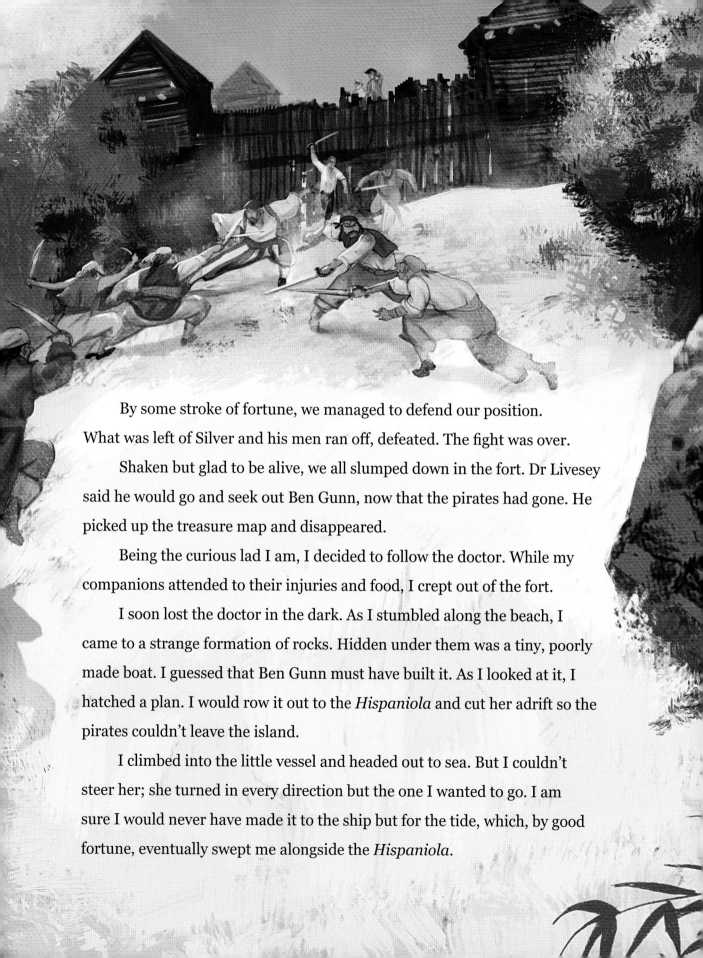

By some stroke of fortune, we managed to defend our position. What was left of Silver and his men ran off, defeated. The fight was over.

Shaken but glad to be alive, we all slumped down in the fort. Dr Livesey said he would go and seek out Ben Gunn, now that the pirates had gone. He picked up the treasure map and disappeared.

Being the curious lad I am, I decided to follow the doctor. While my companions attended to their injuries and food, I crept out of the fort.

I soon lost the doctor in the dark. As I stumbled along the beach, I came to a strange formation of rocks. Hidden under them was a tiny, poorly made boat. I guessed that Ben Gunn must have built it. As I looked at it, I hatched a plan. I would row it out to the *Hispaniola* and cut her adrift so the pirates couldn't leave the island.

I climbed into the little vessel and headed out to sea. But I couldn't steer her; she turned in every direction but the one I wanted to go. I am sure I would never have made it to the ship but for the tide, which, by good fortune, eventually swept me alongside the *Hispaniola*.

I grabbed the anchor rope, hauled myself up and clambered onto the deck. The ship was eerily quiet. I could see two pirates lying in a pool of blood. One was definitely dead. The other groaned and muttered, "Rum!"

It was Israel Hands, Silver's second-in-command.

Hands looked at me slyly. "What are you doing here, boy?"

"I've come to take possession of this ship, and you'll please regard me as your captain until further notice," I replied, faking more courage than I felt.

Hands grimaced at me. "I reckon, Cap'n Hawkins, you'll be wanting to get ashore now. S'pose we strike a deal. I can help you sail this ship back to the island."

It seemed to me that there was some sense in this plan, so we set sail. But, as we neared the shoreline, Hands suddenly lunged at me. I clambered up the rigging to escape.

"Stand down!" I cried, as I pointed my pistol down at him.

Hands roared and hurled his dagger at me. The blade knocked me on the shoulder. As I cried out, my pistol accidentally went off. Hands screamed and plunged head first into the sea.

Shaking, but fortunately not seriously injured, I dropped gently overboard and swam to shore. I was eager to get back to my friends.

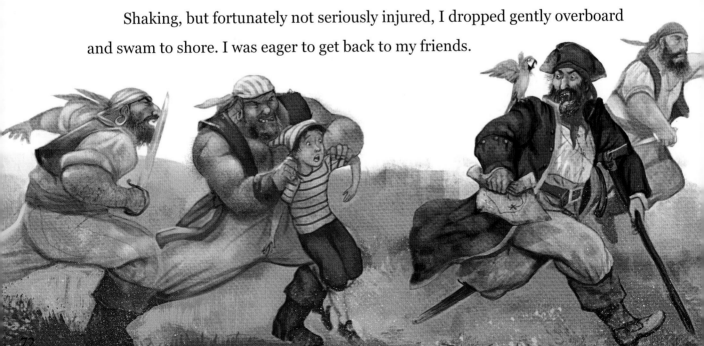

# TREASURE ISLAND

It was dark by the time I reached the fort. With a sigh of relief, I crept inside. Then a pair of hands grabbed me. I was surrounded by pirates!

"Hello, Jim," laughed Silver. "I've always liked you, lad. You've got spirit. As you can see, your friends are gone. You'll have to join up with ol' Cap'n Silver now. And I've got the treasure map!"

I gasped. How had he got the map? And what had happened to my friends?

The next day, Silver announced that the pirates were going treasure hunting and that he was taking me with them so I couldn't escape. Flint's map said his treasure was buried under a tall tree below a hill.

As we neared the place marked with a red cross on the map, one of the men ahead started shouting. The other pirates ran towards him. At the foot of a big pine tree lay a human skeleton.

We were staring at this gruesome sight when, all of a sudden, out of the trees in front of us, a high, trembling voice struck up with the words, "Fifteen men on the dead man's chest, yo-ho-ho, and a bottle of rum!"

I have never seen men more dreadfully affected than the pirates. "It's the ghost of Cap'n Flint!" cried one of the men.

Silver managed to gather his courage. "Lads, it's someone trying to scare us. Come, let's find this treasure."

Up ahead was another tall tree. "That's the spot, lads!" cried Silver. But, as we approached the tree, we could see a great big hole in the ground below it. Silver let out a low groan. Flint's treasure had been found by someone else!

"You dragged us all this way, and for what?" one of the pirates roared as he pointed his pistol at Silver.

But, just then, three shots flashed out of the nearby thicket, and Dr Livesey and Ben Gunn came rushing out of the trees. The terrified pirates ran off.

Silver, however, stayed where he was. "Thank you kindly, doctor," he laughed. "You came in the nick of time for me and Jim! If you'll take me from this cursed island, I'll cause you no further troubles!"

The doctor nodded his agreement, quietly planning to turn Silver over to the authorities once we got back to Bristol.

As we set off towards the rest of the group, Dr Livesey filled us in on what had happened. Ben Gunn, it seemed, had found the treasure several years before, dug it up and hidden it in a cave.

I was very relieved to see all my friends again and even happier when, a few days later, after having transported all the treasure to the *Hispaniola*, we lifted the anchor and left that ill-fated island behind.

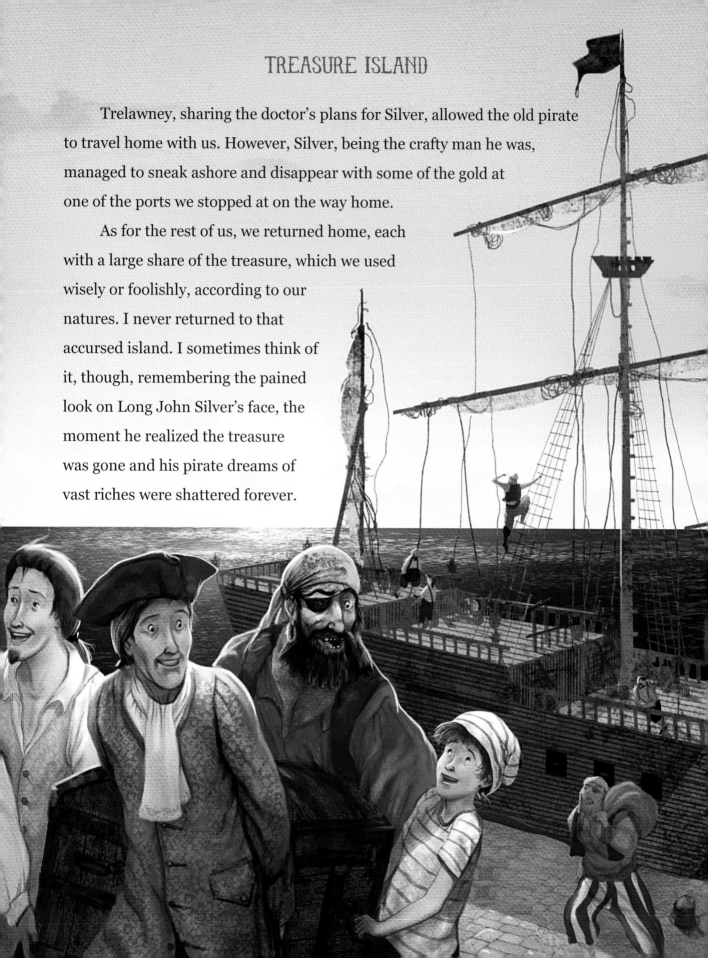

# TREASURE ISLAND

Trelawney, sharing the doctor's plans for Silver, allowed the old pirate to travel home with us. However, Silver, being the crafty man he was, managed to sneak ashore and disappear with some of the gold at one of the ports we stopped at on the way home.

As for the rest of us, we returned home, each with a large share of the treasure, which we used wisely or foolishly, according to our natures. I never returned to that accursed island. I sometimes think of it, though, remembering the pained look on Long John Silver's face, the moment he realized the treasure was gone and his pirate dreams of vast riches were shattered forever.

# BLACK BEAUTY

When I was a very young foal, I lived in a pleasant meadow with a pond of clear water in it. In the daytime, I ran by my mother's side, and, at night, I lay down close beside her. She was a wise old horse and used to tell me, "I hope you will grow up gentle and good, and never learn bad ways. Do your work with a good will, lift your feet up well when you trot and never bite or kick even in play." I have never forgotten her advice.

Our master was a kind man. He gave us good food and good lodging, and he spoke as kindly to us as he did to his own children. We were all fond of him.

I began to grow handsome: my coat was fine, soft and black, and I had one white foot and a pretty white star on my forehead. My master broke me in himself, rather than leave it to one of his grooms. With a good deal of coaxing, oats, pats and gentle words, he taught me to wear a saddle and bridle and to carry a man, woman or child on my back, to go quietly, just the way they wished, and to pull a carriage by holding a bit. I didn't like the bit at all at first – it was a nasty thing to have cold metal in my mouth – but my mother always wore one when she went out, so at last I got used to wearing it.

My mother always told me the better I behaved, the better I would be treated and that I should always do my best to please my master. "I hope you will fall into good hands," she said, "but a horse never knows who may buy him or who may drive him. It is all a chance for us, but still I say, do your best wherever you are, and keep up your good name."

I was four years old when I was sold and taken to Birtwick Park. I was put in a clean, airy stable with a friendly little grey pony and a tall chestnut mare with a long, handsome neck. The groom, John Manly, seemed very proud of me and called me Black Beauty. He would talk to me a great deal. Of course, I did not understand all he said, but I began to learn what he meant and what he wanted me to do. James Howard, the stable boy, was just as gentle and pleasant, so I thought myself well off.

# BLACK BEAUTY

A few days after my arrival, I had to go out with the chestnut mare, Ginger, in the carriage. Ginger had a habit of biting and snapping, so I wondered how we would get on together. But, except for angrily laying her ears back when I was first led up to her, she behaved very well. After we had been out together a few times, she told me her story. It was so different from my own. Ginger had been taken from her mother as soon as she was weaned. She was then broken in by force, with no kind words from her master, and sold to a fashionable gentleman. This man held his horses' heads up with a check-rein, a special type of rein that stopped horses from lowering their heads.

"I had to hold my head up for hours at a time, not able to move it at all," explained Ginger, her nostrils flaring at the memory. "My master thought it looked stylish. I was ready and willing to work, but to be tormented for nothing but his fancy angered me. So I began to snap and kick. Of course, it is very different at Birtwick Park, but who knows how long it will last?"

I felt sorry for Ginger, but I knew very little then. As the weeks rolled on, Ginger grew much more gentle and cheerful, and she lost the nervous, angry look that she used to give to strangers.

After I had been living at Birtwick Park for some months, my master and mistress decided to visit some friends who lived a two-day drive away. Ginger and I were harnessed up, and James drove the carriage. We travelled the whole of the first day and, just as the sun was going down, we reached a hotel, and Ginger and I were put in the stables to spend the night.

Later that evening, a young man smoking a pipe came into the stable. He chatted to the groom, then went into the loft to bring down some hay. Then the man and groom left the stable and locked the door for the night.

I cannot say how long I slept, but, when I awoke, the air was thick and choking with smoke. Low crackling and snapping sounds made me tremble all over. The other horses in the stalls pulled at their halters and stamped in terror.

At last a groom rushed in and began to untie us and lead us out. But he seemed in such a hurry and was so frightened himself that he scared us more. None of us wanted to go with him. Then I heard a cry of "Fire!" outside, and James quickly came in. He quietly took off his scarf and tied it tightly over my eyes so I couldn't see anything that might scare me. Patting and coaxing, James led me out of the stable to safety. Then he went back in to save Ginger. Smoke poured out and I could see flashes of red light. Then I heard a crash as something fell inside. The next moment, James came through the smoke leading Ginger. She was coughing violently and James was unable to speak, but, luckily, they were all right.

That young man had left his pipe in the hayloft and it had set the stable on fire. Thanks to James, Ginger and I were saved. But two of the horses inside could not be brought to safety. It was a terrible night.

After three happy years at Birtwick Park, sad changes came over us.

One night I was fast asleep when the groom, John Manly, ran into the stable and cried, "Wake up, Beauty! Your mistress is near to death and we must fetch the doctor. There is not a moment to lose."

Away we went, out into the night. "Now, Beauty, do your best," said John, and so I did. I don't believe that my old grandfather, who won the race at Newmarket, could have gone faster!

# BLACK BEAUTY

The church clock struck three as we drew up at Dr White's door. His own horse was exhausted by a hard day's riding, so, even though I was tired myself, there was no option but for me to take the doctor back to the Hall.

The doctor was a heavier man than John and not such a good rider. However, I did my very best. When we got home, my legs shook under me, and I could only stand and pant. I had not a dry hair on my body! The doctor went into the house, and Joe, a new stable boy, took charge of me. Poor Joe! He was young and, as yet, he knew very little. He didn't put a warm cloth on me when he should have, as he thought I was hot and would not like it. Then he gave me cold water to drink, which tasted good but chilled my stomach. Soon I began to shake and tremble. By the time John returned, having walked home from the doctor's house, I had turned deadly cold. I was sick for weeks afterwards, and John nursed me night and day.

My mistress recovered but, shortly afterwards, we heard that she must leave England for a warmer country for the sake of her health. My master had to sell everything, including all his horses.

On our last day together, Ginger and I sadly carried the master and mistress on their final journey to the railway station, where they said goodbye to us. Then we drove slowly home – but it was not our home now.

# BLACK BEAUTY

Ginger and I were sold to a gentleman who lived in a fine house called Earlshall Park. When John delivered us to our new stables, he told the groom that he had never used a check-rein on either of us. "Well," said the groom, "they must wear the check-rein here. My lady will have style, and if her carriage horses are not reined up tight, she won't look at them."

I held my face close to John's – that was all I could do to say goodbye – and then he was gone.

The next afternoon we were hitched to the carriage with our heads held up by the check-rein. When my lady appeared, she looked at us and did not seem pleased, but she said nothing and got into the carriage. Though it certainly was a nuisance, the rein was bearable for me. I felt anxious about Ginger, but she seemed to be quiet and content.

Over the next few days, however, my lady insisted that our heads were reined higher and higher, and I began to understand what Ginger had told me. I wanted to put my head forwards and pull the carriage with a will as we had been used to do, but I couldn't, and that took all the spirit out of me and put strain on my back and legs. "If they rein me up tight," said Ginger, "why, let 'em look out! I can't bear it, and I won't."

Finally, it became too much for Ginger. When the groom tried to tighten her reins, she reared up so suddenly that he had his nose roughly hit and his hat knocked off. She was never put with the carriage again. As for me, I was simply given a fresh partner. What I suffered with that rein for four months in my lady's carriage is hard to describe. The sharp bit made me froth at the mouth, and there was a pressure on my windpipe, which often made my breathing very uncomfortable. There was no relief.

# BLACK BEAUTY

I must now say a little about Reuben Smith, who was left in charge of the stables when the groom went to London on the master's business. Reuben was gentle in his management of horses, but he had one great fault: a forgetful and careless nature. Reuben had nearly lost his job in the past because of his lazy ways, and he had promised faithfully that he would be more responsible. I was unlucky enough to be in his care when he got careless again.

One spring day, he left me at the hotel stables while he ran errands in town. He told the groom to have me ready for him at four o'clock, but it was nearly nine o'clock when he called for me, having run into friends and lost track of time. A nail in one of my front shoes had started to come loose, and the groom told Reuben that it needed looking at. Reuben was too hurried to care, so we set off into the night without further delay. He urged me into a gallop, and we travelled far and fast. At last my shoe came off. Reuben did not notice, and my shoeless foot suffered dreadfully. The hoof was split and the inside flesh was cut.

No horse can keep his footing under such circumstances! I stumbled and fell on both my knees, and Reuben was flung off with great force.

After one slight effort to rise, he did not move again. We were far from any town, and it was nearly midnight before men came from Earlshall to find out what had become of us.

Reuben Smith died that night, poor man. Because of his rough riding, my knees were scarred and ugly, and I was no longer fit to work in a gentleman's stables. I was sold and taken from Earlshall without even having a chance to say goodbye to Ginger.

# BLACK BEAUTY

I became a job-horse, which means that I was hired out to all sorts of people. As I was good-tempered and gentle, I think I was more often let out to ignorant drivers than some of the other horses, because I could be depended upon.

One day, I went out in a carriage with a careless driver who let the reins lie easily on my back, while his own hands rested lazily on his knees. There were loose stones on the road, but he never thought it worthwhile to drive on the smooth parts. The result was that I got a stone in my foot. Any good driver would have seen immediately that something was wrong. But this man was laughing and talking with his passengers, and, with every step, the stone became more firmly wedged in my foot. The driver finally noticed I was limping and complained that I was lame.

Just then a farmer rode up and said, "I beg your pardon, sir, but your horse looks as if he has a stone in his shoe. If you will allow me, I will look at his foot."

Sure enough, the farmer found the offending stone, carefully dislodged it with a stone-pick and showed it to the driver.

"Well!" said my driver. "I never knew that horses picked up stones before!"

"Didn't you?" said the farmer, rather scornfully. "They do, and if you don't want to lame your horse, you must look sharp and get them out quickly. If I might advise, sir, you had better drive him gently for a while. The foot is a good deal hurt."

# BLACK BEAUTY

Then, mounting his own horse and raising his hat, the farmer trotted off.

My driver began to flop the reins about as before, so I knew that I was to go on. And, of course, I did, glad at least that the farmer knew about horses and that the stone was gone.

# BLACK BEAUTY

After some months of working in this way, I was put up for sale at a horse fair. No doubt such a place is very amusing to those who have nothing to lose. At any rate, there is plenty to see.

There were long strings of young horses from the country, shaggy little Welsh ponies, hundreds of cart horses of all sorts, with their long tails braided up and tied with scarlet cord, and a good many like myself, handsome and high-bred, but who had suffered an accident or had some blemish. There were some splendid horses, in their prime and fit for anything, but in the background there were a number of poor animals, broken down by hard work. These were sad sights for a horse to look upon and wonder if he may come to be in the same state. I was put with some useful-looking horses, and a good many people came to look at us. The gentlemen always turned from me when they saw my scarred knees.

# BLACK BEAUTY

There was one man who seemed interested in me, and I could tell that I would be happy with him. He was not a gentleman. He was rather a small man and quick in all his movements. I knew in a moment, by the way he handled me, that he was used to horses. He spoke gently, and his grey eyes had a kind, cheery look in them.

He offered twenty-three pounds for me, but that was refused. Then a very hard-looking, loud-voiced man came. I was dreadfully afraid this man would buy me. I could not help reaching out my head towards the grey-eyed man. He stroked my face gently. "Well, old chap," he said, "I think we'll suit each other."

He paid twenty-four pounds on the spot and, half an hour later, we were on our way to London, through pleasant lanes and country roads, till in the twilight we reached the great city.

# BLACK BEAUTY

My new master was Jeremiah Baker but, as everyone called him Jerry, I will do the same. He was married to Polly, and they had two children: Harry, who was nearly twelve years old, and Dorothy, or Dolly as they called her, who was eight. Jerry had a cab and drove two horses, one in the mornings and one in the afternoons. In this way, each horse got a proper rest. And he never worked on a Sunday. It was his golden rule. Even when his most loyal customers asked him to work then, he would say, "I used to work seven days, but it was too hard for me and too hard for my horses. They need rest, and I need to spend Sunday with my wife and children."

The first week of my life as a cab horse was very trying. I was not used to London, and the noise, the hurry, the crowds of horses, carts and carriages made me feel anxious and harassed. But I soon found that I could trust my driver, and then I relaxed and got used to the bustle of the city. In a short time, my master and I understood each other as well as a man and a horse could ever do.

Jerry was a good driver, and, even better, he thought as much for his horses as he did for himself. He soon found out that I was willing to work and do my best, and I believe his whip was more frequently at rest by his side than in his hand. In the stable, too, he did all that he could for our comfort. He kept us very clean and gave us as much change of food as he could, and always plenty of it. Not only that, but he always made sure we had enough clean, fresh water for both night and day. But the very best thing of all was our Sundays of rest.

# BLACK BEAUTY

One day, while we were waiting outside one of the parks, a shabby old cab drove up beside ours. The horse was an old worn-out chestnut, with an ill-kept coat and bones that showed plainly through it. The horse's knees knuckled over and her fore legs were very unsteady. There was a hopeless look in her eyes that I could not help noticing. Then, as I was wondering where I had seen that horse before, she looked straight at me and said, "Black Beauty, is that you?"

It was Ginger, but how she had changed! Her neck was lank, her legs were swollen, her joints were grown out of shape with hard work, and her face, once so full of spirit and life, was now full of suffering. Our drivers were standing together a little way off, so I sidled up to her so that we might have a little quiet talk. It was a sad tale that she had to tell.

Ginger was sold the year after I left Earshall. For a while, all was well, but then her breathing got bad – no doubt the result of being reined up so tightly in her youth – and she was sold again and again, until she was bought by a man who kept cabs and horses and hired them out.

"You look well off, and I am glad of it," said Ginger, "but I could not tell you what my life has been. They work me hard all the week with not a day's rest."

I was very much troubled and I put my nose up to hers. But I could say nothing to comfort her. Just then her driver appeared and, with a tug at her mouth, he drove her away.

A short time after this, a cart with a dead horse in it passed our cabstand. It was a chestnut horse with a long, thin neck. I believe it was Ginger. I hope it was, for then her troubles would have been over.

There came a day when Jerry and I did work on a Sunday, and this is how it happened.

One Sunday morning, Jerry was cleaning me in the yard when his wife, Polly, rushed up to him.

"My dear," she said, "my friend Dinah Brown has just had a letter to say that her mother is dangerously ill, and she must go to her immediately. She lives more than ten miles away, out in the country. The train doesn't take Dinah all the way there so she would have a long walk, with her young baby too. She asks if you would take her in your cab."

"Well, Polly, you know it goes against my golden rule," said Jerry hesitantly, "but we should do for other people as we would like them to do for us, so you may tell Dinah that I'll be ready for her at ten."

I was chosen for the job, and at ten o'clock on the dot we started out. It was a fine May day, and the sweet country air was as good in my nostrils as it was in the old days.

When we reached Dinah's family home, which was a small farmhouse close by a meadow, a young man offered to tie me up in the cowshed, apologizing that he had no better stable to offer.

"That's kind," said Jerry, "but there is nothing my horse would like so well as to have an hour or two in your beautiful meadow. It would be a rare treat for him."

The young man happily agreed to this plan. When my harness was taken off, I did not know what I should do first: whether to eat the grass, or roll over on my back, or lie down and rest, or have a gallop across the meadow out of sheer spirits at being free. So I did them all by turns! Jerry seemed to be quite as happy as I was and took it easy under a shady tree until it was time for us to take Dinah back to London.

# BLACK BEAUTY

The following Christmas and New Year were very merry for some people, but for me and my master, they brought sadness and a parting. Late-night working, with snow, sleet or heavy rain every day, took its toll on us both. Jerry caught bronchitis and became dangerously ill. When he got better, his doctor said that he must never go back to cab work if he wished to be an old man. So Jerry and the family moved to the country, where he took a job as a coachman. His cab and horses were sold. It was the saddest day of all for me.

At the horse sale, I now found myself in the company of the old, lame and sick horses. After three years of cab work, I was not the horse that I had been. Many men looked at me and turned away. Then an old gentleman approached with a young boy by his side. I saw his eye rest on me, and I pricked my ears and looked at him.

"There's a horse, Willie, that has known better days," he said to the boy.

"Poor old fellow! Could not you buy him and make him young again, as you did with our horse, Ladybird?" asked the boy.

The old gentleman laughed. Then he felt my legs, looked at my mouth and asked to see me trot around. To my great joy, he bought me for five pounds.

And that is how I came to my last home. The old gentleman gave me to three ladies in the neighbourhood who needed a good, safe horse to pull their carriage. And their groom turned out to be Joe Green, the stable boy at Birtwick Park from all those years ago, now a confident young man.

I have been living in this happy place a whole year. Joe is the best of grooms, clever and with always a kind word. My work is easy, and my strength and spirit are returning. My ladies have promised that I shall never be sold, and so I have nothing to fear. So here my story ends.

# THE SECRET GARDEN

Mary Lennox was the most disagreeable-looking child ever seen. She had been born in India and had always been ill. Her father had always been busy and ill himself, and her mother had not wanted a little girl at all. When Mary was born, her mother handed her over to the care of the servants. As the servants always obeyed Mary, she became very selfish.

# THE SECRET GARDEN

One hot morning, when she was about nine years old, Mary woke to find an unfamiliar servant by her bedside. The woman would not bring Mary's Ayah, her usual nanny, and so Mary threw herself into a tantrum and hit and kicked the woman.

When no one would tell her anything, Mary wandered outside and played under a tree, pretending to make a garden. She heard her mother talking on the veranda with a young army officer. The disease cholera had broken out, and Mary's Ayah had just died. Later that same day, three other servants died, and all the others ran away in terror.

The next day, Mary hid in the nursery and was forgotten by everyone. The house grew more and more silent. Mary was standing in the middle of the nursery when a strange man opened the door. He was horrified to see her, but Mary was only cross.

"I am Mary Lennox. I fell asleep when everyone had the cholera. Why was I forgotten?" She stamped her foot.

"Poor little child!" he said. "There is nobody left to come."

In that strange way Mary found out that she had neither father nor mother left. There was no one in the bungalow but herself.

She was sent by ship to England to live with her uncle, Mr Archibald Craven, at Misselthwaite Manor. When they landed, the officer's wife who had looked after her on the ship was very glad to hand the cross little thing over to Mr Craven's housekeeper, Mrs Medlock. The housekeeper was a stout woman, with very red cheeks and sharp black eyes. Mary thought her the most disagreeable person she had ever seen.

# THE SECRET GARDEN

After the ship, they took a train for a very long time. Mary sat in her corner of the carriage looking plain and fretful.

"You are going to an odd place," Mrs Medlock told her. "The house is six hundred years old and on the edge of the moor. There's near a hundred rooms in it. Mr Craven won't trouble himself about you. Most of the time he goes away, and when he's here, he shuts himself up and won't let anyone see him. He's got a crooked back and was a sour young man till he married a sweet, pretty thing. Then she died – and now he cares about nobody. You mustn't expect anyone to talk to you much."

The train took such a long time that Mary fell asleep. She awoke to find Mrs Medlock shaking her. They had stopped at a station, and a smart carriage stood waiting for them. It rattled through the dark over wild land that had no trees or hedges.

At last, they stopped in front of a long, low house built round a stone courtyard. Mrs Medlock led Mary to a room with a lit fire and supper on a table.

"Well, here you are!" Mrs Medlock said. "This room and the next are where you'll live – and you must keep to them. Don't you forget that!"

# THE SECRET GARDEN

When Mary opened her eyes in the morning, a young housemaid was cleaning the fireplace. Out of the window, Mary could see a great stretch of land with no trees on it. It looked like an endless, dull, purplish sea.

"That's th' moor," said Martha, the housemaid, in what Mary thought was a very strange accent. "Does tha' like it?"

"No," answered Mary. "I hate it."

"That's because tha'rt not used to it," Martha said. "But tha' will like it."

"Who is going to dress me?" demanded Mary.

"Canna' tha' dress thyself?" Martha said.

"What do you mean? I don't understand your language," snapped Mary.

"I mean, can't you put on your own clothes?"

"No," answered Mary. "I never did in my life. My servants dressed me."

"Well," said Martha, "it's time tha' should learn. It'll do thee good to wait on thyself a bit." Mary could scarcely stand this.

At first, Mary was not at all interested in Martha. But, after a few minutes, she began to take notice as Martha talked about her home, her eleven brothers and sisters and how they played all day on the moor.

"Our Dickon, he's twelve, and he's got a young pony. He found it on th' moor. And it got to like him so it follows him about an' lets him get on its back. Dickon's a kind lad, an' animals like him."

Mary began to feel a slight curiosity about Dickon.

In the nursery, a table was set with a good-sized breakfast. But Mary ate only a little toast and some marmalade.

After breakfast, Martha told her to put on her coat and play outside.

"Our Dickon goes off on th' moor by himself an' plays for hours. That's how he made friends with th' pony."

Martha told her how to get to the gardens. She seemed to hesitate a second before she added that there was a garden that no one had been in for ten years – a garden that had been beautiful and full of roses, but was now locked up and forgotten.

"Why?" asked Mary in spite of herself.

"Mr Craven had it shut when his wife died. It was her garden. He locked th' door an' dug a hole and buried th' key. Now, out you go to play."

As Mary walked through the walled gardens, she could not help thinking about the garden that no one had been in for ten years.

She followed paths and went through doors until she saw an old man with a spade over his shoulder. He looked startled when he saw Mary.

"What is that?" said Mary, pointing to a green door.

"Another garden. There's another t'other side o' th' wall an' there's th' orchard t'other side o' that."

Mary went through to the orchard. She could see the tops of trees above a wall and a bird with a bright red breast sitting on one of them. Suddenly the bird burst into song. She walked back to the old man.

"I went in the orchard. There was no door into the garden over the wall. But there are trees there – I saw a bird with a red breast sitting on one of them."

The man whistled, and the bird landed near his foot.

"What kind of a bird is he?" Mary asked.

"Doesn't tha' know? He's a robin redbreast. And I'm Ben Weatherstaff. Art tha' th' little girl from India?"

Mary nodded. The gardener jerked his thumb towards the robin. "He's th' only friend I've got."

"I have no friends. Would you make friends with me?" Mary asked the robin.

"Why," Ben cried, "tha' said that almost like Dickon talks to his wild things."

The robin flew over the wall.

"He lives there," said Ben. "Among th' old rose trees."

"Rose trees?" said Mary. "I should like to see them. There must be a door somewhere."

"None as anyone can find, an' none as is anyone's business. Get you gone an' play. I've no more time."

The next day, Mary ate a little breakfast and realized that if she did not go out, she would have to stay in and do nothing – so she went out.

She hated the wind, but the fresh air filled her lungs and whipped red into her cheeks. Mary began to stay out of doors nearly all day, day after day, and when she sat down to her supper at night, she felt hungry. She was not cross when Martha chattered away and rather liked to hear her. One windy night she asked Martha why Mr Craven hated the garden so much. Martha told her that Mrs Craven had died there ten years ago, when a branch she used to sit on broke. Mary looked at the fire and listened to the wind howling outside. But she began to hear something else.

"Do you hear anyone crying?" she asked.

"No," Martha answered. "It's th' wind. Sometimes it sounds like someone lost on th' moor an' wailin'."

"But listen," said Mary. "It's in the house."

"It is th' wind," said Martha stubbornly. But Mary did not believe she was speaking the truth.

The next day the rain poured down, and Mary spent the morning wandering the house. She lost her way two or three times, but at last she reached her own floor again. Then she heard a cry.

She put her hand on the tapestry near her. It covered a door which fell open into a corridor. Mrs Medlock was coming down it with a very cross look on her face. She pulled Mary away by the arm.

"I turned round the wrong corner," explained Mary. "And I heard someone crying."

"You didn't hear anything of the sort. You come along back to your own nursery or I'll give you a slap."

And she dragged her to her own room.

Mary sat on the rug, pale with rage.

"There was someone crying – there was!" she said to herself.

Two days later, Mary went back to the gardens and saw the robin hopping about, pretending to peck things out of a pile of earth. He pointed at something almost buried in the soil – an old key! Mary uncovered it and hid it in her pocket when she went back to the house for dinner.

Next day, she said to the robin, "You showed me where the key was yesterday. Please show me the door today!"

Just then, a gust of wind blew aside the ivy, and Mary saw the knob of a door which had been closed for ten years. She put the key in, turned it slowly and pushed hard on the door. Then she slipped through, shutting the door behind her.

She was standing inside the secret garden. The high walls were covered with leafless rose stems matted together. The branches had run all over the trees, swaying together like curtains.

Mary felt as if she had found a world all her own. She saw the sharp little pale green points of growing plants and wondered if they might be crocuses or snowdrops or daffodils. The grass seemed so thick that some did not seem to have room to grow. So she took a sharp piece of wood and dug the weeds and grass, clearing space until it was time for her midday dinner.

"I wish I had a little spade," Mary said to Martha at dinner. "Then I could dig somewhere and make a little garden."

Martha knew a shop that sold little garden sets and seeds. She helped Mary write to Dickon asking him to buy them and bring them over – Mary had enough money of her own, as each week she was given a little from Mr Craven.

Mary was beginning to like being out of doors; she no longer hated the wind. She worked and dug and pulled up weeds steadily every day.

One day when Mary went outside, a boy was sitting under a tree playing a wooden pipe. On the trunk of the tree was a brown squirrel, and two rabbits sat nearby.

"I'm Dickon," the boy said. "And I know tha'rt Miss Mary."

He had brought the tools and seeds and asked where her garden was.

"Could you keep a secret?" she said. "I've stolen a garden. Nobody cares for it. Nobody ever goes into it."

She lifted the hanging ivy, and they passed in together. Dickon stood looking round him.

"I never thought I'd see this place," he said.

"Did you know about it?" asked Mary. Dickon nodded.

Then he showed Mary that the stems of the roses had green inside them so were still alive. They began to work harder than ever, and Mary was sorry when she heard the clock strike for midday dinner.

There was a surprise waiting for her when she returned to the house: Mr Craven had come back and wanted to see her. Mrs Medlock took her down the corridors to a part of the house she had not been in before. A man with high, crooked shoulders was sitting before the fire. He looked as if he did not know what in the world to do with her.

"Are you well?" he finally asked.

"Yes," answered Mary.

"Do they take good care of you?"

"Yes."

"You are very thin," he said. He looked at her closely. "Don't look so frightened. Is there anything you want?"

"Might I," quavered Mary, "have a bit of earth to plant seeds?"

"You can have as much earth as you want," he said. "When you see a bit you want, take it, child – make it come alive." He paused, then said, "Now, you must go. I am tired."

That night, Mary woke to a strange sound. "That isn't the wind," she whispered. "I am going to find out what it is. I don't care about Mrs Medlock. I don't care!"

She crept down the shadowy corridors, led by the far-off crying, until she found a big room she had never been to before. A thin, pale boy lay in a bed.

"Are you a ghost?" he said in a frightened voice when she entered.

"No," Mary answered. "Are you?"

"No," he replied. "I am Colin Craven. Mr Craven is my father."

No one had told Mary that Mr Craven had a son.

Colin told her that he was always ill. "If I live, I may have a crooked back and be a hunchback like my father. But I shan't live," he said. "My mother died around the time I was born, and it makes my father wretched to look at me."

"He hates the garden, because she died," said Mary, half speaking to herself.

"What garden?" Colin asked.

"Oh! Just – just a garden she used to like," Mary stammered.

He made her tell him about India and about her voyage across the ocean. And he told her about himself – how everyone had to do what he said because being angry made him ill.

"How old are you?" he asked.

"I am ten," answered Mary, "and so are you, because when you were born, the garden door was locked and the key was buried. And it has been locked for ten years."

"What garden door was locked? Where was the key buried?" he exclaimed.

"Mr Craven locked the door," said Mary. "No one knew where he buried the key."

Colin said he would force the servants to take him there. But Mary knew that would spoil everything! She promised that she would find a way for them to go together – then it would stay a secret garden.

The next day, Mary crept back to see Colin. She told him all about Dickon: how he could charm foxes and squirrels and birds, and how he knew everything on the moor.

"I couldn't go on the moor," Colin said. "How could I? I am going to die."

Mary didn't like the way he talked about dying. He almost boasted about it. So she continued talking about the garden. They were laughing about Ben Weatherstaff and the robin, when Colin's doctor and Mrs Medlock walked in. They jumped in alarm, but then Colin introduced Mary.

"She makes me better," he said.

And so Mary was allowed to see Colin from then on.

For a week the weather was bad, but finally the sky was blue. Mary flew downstairs and out to the secret garden. Dickon was already there, working hard. Mary was so happy to meet his fox cub and his tame rook, Soot, that she could hardly breathe. She told him about Colin.

"If he was out here, he wouldn't be watchin' for lumps on his back," said Dickon. "It'd be good for him. Us'd be just two children watchin' a garden grow, an' he'd be another."

When Mary went to see Colin later, he was angry. He said he would send Dickon away if he kept Mary from him.

"If you send Dickon away, I'll never come again!" she retorted. "You're the most selfish boy I ever saw."

"I'm not as selfish as you," snapped Colin, "because I'm always ill, and I'm going to die."

"You're not!" said Mary sourly. "You just say that to make people sorry."

"Get out of the room!" he shouted.

"I'm going," she said. "And I won't come back!"

In the middle of the night, Mary was awakened by dreadful screaming and crying. Just then, Colin's nurse came in and begged her to go to Colin. Mary flew along the corridor.

"You stop!" she shouted at Colin. "I hate you! Everybody hates you! You will scream yourself to death in a minute, and I wish you would!"

"I can't stop!" he sobbed.

"You can!" shouted Mary. "Half that ails you is temper!"

"I felt the lump," choked out Colin. "I shall have a hunch on my back and die!"

"There's nothing the matter with your horrid back!" contradicted Mary. "If you ever say there is again, I shall laugh!"

Mary demanded the nurse show her Colin's back.

"There's not a single lump there!" said Mary at last. "There's not a lump as big as a pin – except normal backbone lumps."

No one but Colin knew what effect those words had on him. Now that an angry, unsympathetic little girl insisted that he was not ill, he actually felt it might be true.

"Do you think – I could – live to grow up?" he said.

The nurse said that Colin's doctor had said he would probably live if he did not give way to temper and if he spent time in the fresh air.

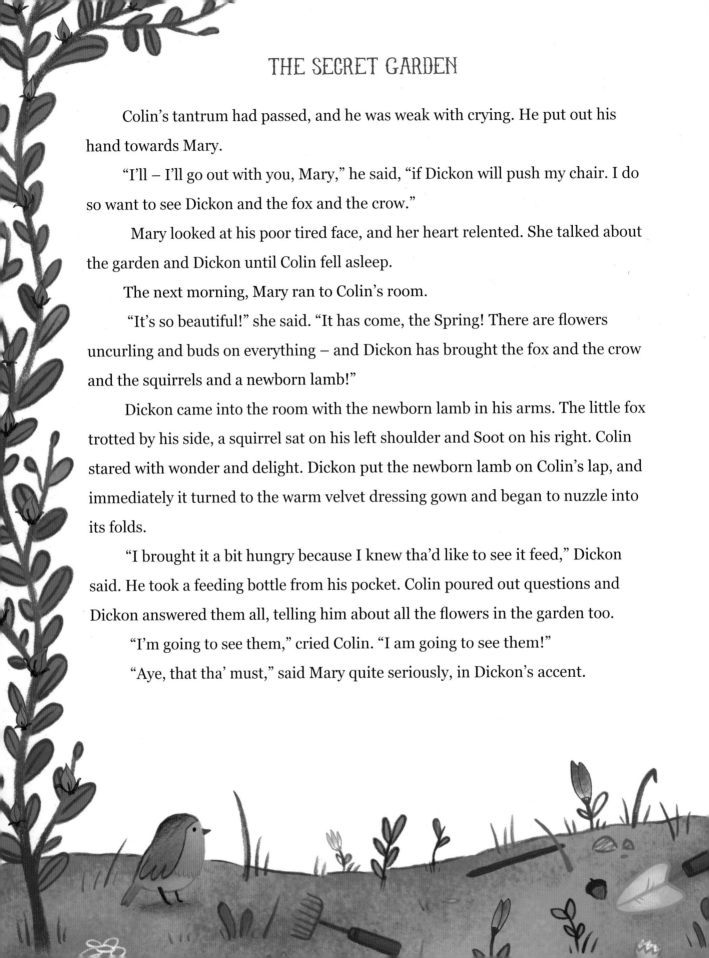

# THE SECRET GARDEN

Colin's tantrum had passed, and he was weak with crying. He put out his hand towards Mary.

"I'll – I'll go out with you, Mary," he said, "if Dickon will push my chair. I do so want to see Dickon and the fox and the crow."

Mary looked at his poor tired face, and her heart relented. She talked about the garden and Dickon until Colin fell asleep.

The next morning, Mary ran to Colin's room.

"It's so beautiful!" she said. "It has come, the Spring! There are flowers uncurling and buds on everything – and Dickon has brought the fox and the crow and the squirrels and a newborn lamb!"

Dickon came into the room with the newborn lamb in his arms. The little fox trotted by his side, a squirrel sat on his left shoulder and Soot on his right. Colin stared with wonder and delight. Dickon put the newborn lamb on Colin's lap, and immediately it turned to the warm velvet dressing gown and began to nuzzle into its folds.

"I brought it a bit hungry because I knew tha'd like to see it feed," Dickon said. He took a feeding bottle from his pocket. Colin poured out questions and Dickon answered them all, telling him about all the flowers in the garden too.

"I'm going to see them," cried Colin. "I am going to see them!"

"Aye, that tha' must," said Mary quite seriously, in Dickon's accent.

# THE SECRET GARDEN

One afternoon, Dickon pushed Colin's wheelchair to the ivied walls of the secret garden.

"This is where the robin showed me the key," said Mary. "And here is the door! Dickon, push him in quickly!"

Little green leaves had now crept over the walls and trees, and in the grass were splashes of gold and purple flowers. The sun fell warm on Colin's face.

"I shall get well!" he cried. "And I shall live forever and ever!"

Mary and Dickon worked, and Colin watched. They brought him things to look at: buds which were opening, the feather of a woodpecker, an empty egg shell. Every moment was full of new things.

"I don't want this afternoon to go," he said, "but I shall come back. I'm going to see everything grow here, and grow here myself!"

They were quiet for a while, then Colin exclaimed, "Who is that man?"

Ben Weatherstaff was glaring over the wall from the top of a ladder!

He shook his fist at Mary and shouted at her. "I never thought much o' thee! Always askin' questions an' pokin' tha' nose where it wasna wanted."

But when he spotted the wheelchair, he stopped shaking his fist and stared, open-mouthed.

"Do you know who I am?" demanded Colin.

Ben Weatherstaff passed his hand over his eyes.

"Aye," he said, "tha'rt th' poor cripple."

"I'm not a cripple!" Colin cried furiously.

Dickon held Colin's arm; the thin legs were out; the thin feet were on the grass. Colin was standing upright – as straight as an arrow!

Mary turned pale. "He can do it! He can do it!" she whispered to herself.

# THE SECRET GARDEN

Ben Weatherstaff choked, and small tears ran down his cheeks.

"Eh! Th' lies folk tells!" he cried.

Colin made Ben Weatherstaff promise to keep their secret. Then Ben helped Colin to plant a rose.

"This is my garden now," Colin said, "and I shall come here every day."

Month after month, the garden grew more beautiful, and Colin grew stronger. One day, they all agreed that Dickon's mother, Susan Sowerby, could share the secret.

"It was a good thing that little lass came to th' Manor," she said. "It's been th' savin o' Colin. What do they make of it at th' Manor?"

"They don't know," answered Dickon. "If the doctor knew, he'd write and tell Mester Craven, and Colin wants to show him hisself."

She laughed when they told her the difficulty in pretending Colin was still a fretful invalid.

"Tha' won't have to keep it up much longer," she said.

During the months that the secret garden was coming alive, Archibald Craven had been travelling in far-away places. One morning he had a letter from Susan Sowerby, asking him to come home.

# THE SECRET GARDEN

In a few days, Mr Craven was back at his manor.

When he arrived, Mrs Medlock told him that Colin was outside. Mr Craven went through the gardens and found himself at his wife's favourite place. The ivy hung thick over the door, and yet there were sounds inside the secret garden like the laughter of children. And then feet ran faster and faster, and the door in the wall was flung wide open. A boy burst through it at full speed and dashed almost into his arms.

He was a tall boy and a handsome one, glowing with life. He threw the thick hair back from his forehead and lifted a pair of strange grey eyes. It was the eyes that made Mr Craven gasp.

"Who? What? Who?" he stammered.

"Father," he said, "I'm Colin. I see you can't believe it. I scarcely can myself! It was the garden that did it – and Mary and Dickon and the creatures. No one knows. We kept it to tell you when you came."

He said it all so like a healthy boy that Mr Craven's soul shook with joy.

"Aren't you glad? I'm going to live forever and ever and ever!" said Colin.

Mr Craven put his hands on the boy's shoulders.

"Take me into the garden, my boy," he said at last. "And tell me all about it."

The place was a wilderness of autumn gold and purple and violet blue and flaming scarlet. Late roses climbed and hung and clustered in the sunshine. He looked round and round.

Then they sat down under a tree – all but Colin, who wanted to stand while he told the story.

Archibald Craven thought it was the strangest thing he had ever heard.

"Now," Colin said, "it need not be a secret any more. I am never going to get into the chair again."

When Mrs Medlock looked out of the window, she shrieked. All the servants came running to see: there was Mr Craven and, by his side, walking as steadily as any boy in Yorkshire, Master Colin. Following closely behind them was Mary, the most agreeable-looking child ever seen.

# OLIVER TWIST

Oliver Twist was born in the workhouse. His mother pressed her cold, white lips against his forehead, fell back – and died.

Oliver found his place at once: an orphan, to be tossed and beaten through the world, despised by all and pitied by none.

As there was no one to look after him, Oliver was sent to live with elderly Mrs Mann. She kept for herself most of the money given to feed children in her care, and many of them died. By Oliver's ninth birthday, he was a pale, thin child. But he had a good, sturdy spirit.

One day, Mr Bumble, the beadle in charge of the workhouse, said, "Oliver Twist is too old to remain here. We have decided to take him back to the workhouse. Will you come along with me, Oliver?"

Mrs Mann gave Oliver a thousand embraces and (what Oliver wanted a great deal more) a piece of bread and butter – in case he seemed hungry when he got to the workhouse, and it looked as if she wasn't taking good care of the children.

As Oliver was led away from the wretched home where he had never had one kind word or look, he burst into an agony of childish grief. His loneliness sank into his heart for the first time. That night, Oliver sobbed himself to sleep on a rough, hard workhouse bed.

The boys in the workhouse were fed in a large, stone hall, with a cauldron at one end. From this, the master ladled gruel, a thin mix of oats and water. Each boy had one small bowl and no more. The bowls never needed washing: the boys polished them with their spoons till they shone again.

# OLIVER TWIST

Finally, the boys were so wild with hunger they decided someone should ask for more. The task fell to Oliver Twist.

The evening arrived. The gruel was served and disappeared; the boys whispered and winked at Oliver. He was desperate with hunger. Advancing to the master, bowl in hand, he said:

"Please, sir, I want some more."

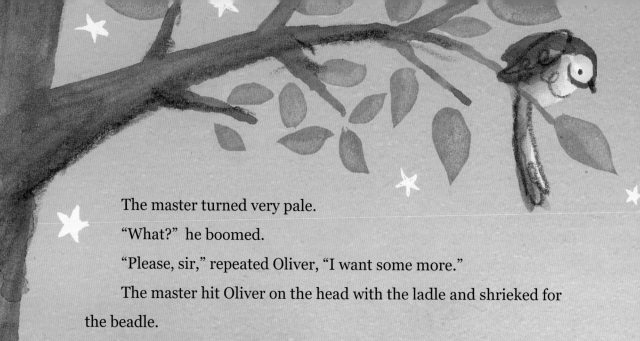

The master turned very pale.

"What?" he boomed.

"Please, sir," repeated Oliver, "I want some more."

The master hit Oliver on the head with the ladle and shrieked for the beadle.

Next morning, a notice was pasted on the gate offering five pounds to anybody who would take Oliver Twist to be an apprentice to any trade. It was soon arranged that he should go to Mr Sowerberry, the undertaker.

"Dear me!" said the undertaker's wife when Oliver arrived. "He's very small."

Charlotte, the maid, led Oliver downstairs and gave Oliver a plateful of coarse, broken scraps of food the dog had left. Oliver tore the bits apart hungrily, eating them quickly.

"Your bed's under the shop counter," said Mrs Sowerberry. "You don't mind sleeping among the coffins, I suppose?"

Oliver gazed about him with dread. An unfinished coffin stood in the middle of the shop, and the space for his mattress looked like a grave.

Mr Sowerberry had an assistant, called Noah Claypole. Noah bullied Oliver. One day, he pulled Oliver's hair and said, "How's your mother?"

"She's dead," replied Oliver.

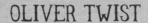

"Yer mother was a regular bad 'un. And it's better that she died when she did, or else she'd have been hung."

Oliver seized Noah by the throat and shook him till his teeth chattered.

"Charlotte! Missis!" blubbered Noah.

Charlotte and Mrs Sowerberry dragged Oliver, struggling and shouting, into the cellar and locked him up for the rest of the day. When he was put back among the coffins for the night, he wept for a long time. Then he tied the little clothing he had into a bundle and, at first light, stepped into the street.

A milestone showed that it was seventy miles to London. London! thought Oliver. Nobody could ever find him there! He walked until his feet were sore and his legs so weak that they trembled. Early on the seventh morning, he limped into the little town of Barnet. He sat on a doorstep, covered with dust and with bleeding feet.

Then one of the strangest-looking boys Oliver had ever seen came up to him.

# OLIVER TWIST

The boy was short, with bowed legs and a stubby nose, and he wore a huge man's coat with the cuffs turned back.

"Hullo, mate! What's going on with you?" he said to Oliver.

"I'm so hungry and tired," replied Oliver.

"I suppose you want somewhere to sleep tonight?" said the strange boy. "Do you have any family?"

"No," said Oliver.

"Stick with me then," said the boy.

Oliver discovered that his new friend's name was Jack Dawkins, but most people called him 'The Artful Dodger'.

When they arrived in London, the Dodger took Oliver to a grim-looking house. The walls and ceiling were black with age and dirt, and Oliver felt anxious, thinking he shouldn't have come. A very old man, with matted red hair, stood frying sausages. Four boys were seated around a table. They grinned at Oliver.

"Fagin," said the Dodger, "this is my friend, Oliver Twist."

The man grinned.

"We're very glad to see you, Oliver," he said, offering him a plate of food.

After breakfast the next day, Fagin, the Dodger and another boy, Charley Bates, played what Oliver thought was a curious game. Fagin trotted up and down the room with a walking stick. The two boys followed him closely and snuck items from him as he walked. If he felt a hand in any of his pockets, Fagin cried out where the hand was, and then the game began all over again.

After a while, the Dodger and Charley went out with two young ladies, named Bet and Nancy.

# OLIVER TWIST

"Is my handkerchief hanging out of my pocket, my dear?" said Fagin to Oliver, when they had gone. "See if you can take it out without my feeling it, as you saw them do this morning."

"Here it is, sir," said Oliver, showing it in his hand.

"You're a clever boy, my dear," said Fagin, patting Oliver on the head.

After many days, Oliver begged Fagin to allow him to go out with Charley and the Dodger. Fagin agreed, and the three boys set off. The Dodger made a sudden stop.

"Do you see that old guy at the bookstall?" he asked. Charley nodded.

The two boys crept close behind the old gentleman.

To Oliver's horror, the Dodger plunged his hand into the gentleman's pocket and drew out a handkerchief! Then the Dodger and Charley ran away at full speed. Oliver made off as fast as he could too. The old gentleman hurried after him, shouting, "Stop, thief!" A crowd followed, and at last Oliver was stopped. A police officer seized him by the collar and dragged him along the streets to the magistrate.

The robbed gentleman, Mr Brownlow, explained he had chased Oliver just because he had seen him running away. But he was a kindly gentleman, and, if it was not Oliver who had robbed him – and he couldn't be sure – he didn't want him to be in trouble.

Just then, Oliver fainted.

"He has been hurt!" Mr Brownlow said. "I fear that he is ill."

An elderly man rushed into the office.

"Wait!" he cried. "The robbery was committed by another boy. I saw it."

Worried about Oliver's health, Mr Brownlow called a coach and took Oliver to his own house in Pentonville.

# OLIVER TWIST

For many days, Oliver lay ill in bed. But at last he was well enough to sit up with the housekeeper, Mrs Bedwin, eating bits of toast broken into broth. He had only been there a few minutes when Mr Brownlow walked in.

"Poor boy!" he said. "How do you feel, my dear?"

"Very happy, sir," replied Oliver. "And very grateful indeed, sir."

"Why! Mrs Bedwin, look!" said the old gentleman.

He pointed to a picture of a woman on the wall and then to Oliver's face. Every feature was the same. Mr Brownlow turned back to Oliver. Now he saw the resemblance to someone once dear to him, he was even more determined to help the boy.

They were happy days, those of Oliver's recovery. Mr Brownlow provided new clothes for him, and Oliver gave his old clothes to a servant to sell.

One day, Mr Brownlow had some books to return to a bookseller. Oliver was keen to be helpful, so Mr Brownlow sent him with the books and a five-pound note to pay the bookseller.

"He'll join his old thieving friends and laugh at you," said Mr Grimwig, a friend who was visiting Mr Brownlow. "If that boy ever returns to this house, I'll eat my head."

But Mr Brownlow trusted that Oliver would return.

# OLIVER TWIST

As Oliver Twist was walking along, he felt a pair of arms thrown tightly around his neck.

"Don't!" cried Oliver, struggling. "Let go of me!"

"Oh, goodness!" said Nancy. "I've found him! Oh! Oliver!"

"Young Oliver!" cried a man. It was Bill Sikes, another of Fagin's gang. "Come home directly!"

"That's not my home!" cried Oliver, struggling. "Help!"

But no help was near. In another moment, Oliver was dragged into a maze of dark, narrow streets.

"Delighted to see you looking so well, my dear," said Fagin when they got to the house. Sikes took the five-pound note from Oliver, and the others took his books and his new clothes off him.

"Oh, pray send back the books and money," begged Oliver. "He'll think I stole them!"

"You're right," remarked Fagin, "he *will* think you have stolen 'em. Ha!"

At first, Oliver was kept locked in a room alone, but after a week, he was allowed to wander about the house. He noticed again how dirty it was, how different from Mr Brownlow's. And he felt desperate at losing the kind affection he had enjoyed there.

"Why don't you work for Fagin?" said Charley.

"I don't like it," said Oliver timidly. "I – I – would rather go."

From that day, Oliver was seldom left alone and was always with the two boys, who played the old game with Fagin every day.

One night, Nancy took Oliver to help Bill Sikes. Bill and Oliver walked for more than a day and a night and eventually came to a house surrounded by a high wall, which they climbed. Oliver realized that they were going to break in.

He sank to his knees. "Oh, let me go!" he cried. "Do not make me steal!"

But Sikes took no notice. He put Oliver through a little window at the back of the house.

"Go along the hall to the door and let me in," whispered Sikes.

Oliver decided to dart upstairs and alert the family.

"Come back!" cried Sikes fiercely.

Scared, Oliver dropped his lantern. Two men appeared at the top of the stairs. There was a flash, a loud noise, smoke – and Oliver staggered back and out of the door.

# OLIVER TWIST

"They've hit him! How the boy bleeds!" Sikes said. He grabbed Oliver by the collar and fired his own pistol at the men. Sikes dragged Oliver from the house and into a field, then left him lying in a ditch and ran. A cold, deadly feeling crept over Oliver's heart, and he saw and heard no more. He lay motionless in the ditch.

Finally, Oliver awoke and staggered to a road. He saw a house and made towards it. As he drew nearer, he saw it was the house they had attempted to rob. He knocked at the door, then collapsed.

The door opened.

"A boy!" exclaimed one of his pursuers from the night before. He dragged Oliver into the hall, calling, "Here's one of the thieves, wounded!"

"Is the poor creature much hurt?" whispered a female voice. She sent for the doctor, Mr Losberne.

As well as a broken and bleeding arm from being shot, Oliver had a fever. He was ill for many weeks, but he eventually grew better under the care of the doctor and the ladies of the house, Mrs Maylie and Rose.

# OLIVER TWIST

"Mr Brownlow would be pleased to know how happy I am," said Oliver one day. So Mr Losberne took him in a carriage to visit Mr Brownlow. But alas! The house was empty. The servant next door told them that Mr Brownlow had gone away.

When the warm weather came, Mrs Maylie, Rose and Oliver went to stay at a cottage in the country. One day, Mrs Maylie sent Oliver to a nearby town with a letter. On his way home, Oliver stumbled against a man in a cloak.

"Ha!" cried the man. "Rot you! I could have got rid of you ages ago! What are you doing here?"

His words meant nothing to Oliver, who gazed in amazement at the madman (for such he supposed he must be) and then returned home.

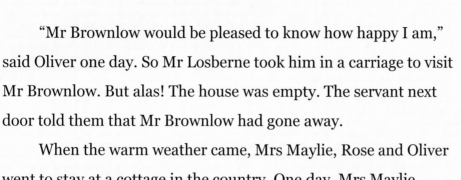

A few days later, Oliver fell asleep at his window and dreamt, with terror, that he was in Fagin's house. Fagin was there, with another man in a large cloak.

"Hush!" Fagin said. "It's him, sure enough."

"Him!" the other man answered. "If you buried him fifteen metres deep and took me across his grave, I should know that he lay buried there."

Oliver awoke. At the window, peering into the room, stood Fagin! And beside him, white with rage, was the strange man he'd bumped into. In an instant, they were gone.

Oliver called for help. Everyone hunted the garden and fields, but in vain.

Meanwhile, back in Oliver's hometown, Mr Bumble had married the woman in charge of the children and staff in the workhouse.

"Are you going to sit there snoring all day?" asked Mrs Bumble one evening. "Be off!" So Mr Bumble went to a public house, where he noticed a man in a large cloak staring at him.

"I've seen you before," said the man. "I want some information from you." He pushed a couple of gold coins across the table. "Think back twelve years. A boy was born in the workhouse..."

"Young Oliver Twist!" said Mr Bumble.

"Yes, I spotted him the other day. Where is the hag that nursed his mother?"

"She died last winter," said Mr Bumble. But he was cunning. Wanting more gold coins, he told the stranger that his wife knew more. They arranged to meet next day.

"What name am I to ask for?" said Mr Bumble.

"Monks!" replied the man, and he strode away.

Mr and Mrs Bumble went next day to meet Monks in an old building by the river.

"You were with this hag the night she died?" Monks said to Mrs Bumble. "And she told you something..."

"About Oliver's mother," she replied. "Yes. Give me five-and-twenty pounds in gold, and I'll tell you all I know."

Monks handed over the gold.

"The nurse and I were alone when she died," Mrs Bumble began. "She said she had stolen gold from Oliver's dead mother. After the nurse died, I found a scrap of dirty paper in her hand – a pawnbroker's ticket. I took it and collected the item."

Mrs Bumble threw a small bag on the table. Monks tore it open, taking little gold locket holding two curls of hair, and a plain gold wedding ring.

"It has 'Agnes' engraved on the inside," said Mrs Bumble.

Monks tugged an iron ring in the floor, pulling up a large trapdoor. Water was rushing rapidly below. He dropped the items into the stream, and they were gone.

"Now get out," he said to the Bumbles. "Go on, go!"

# OLIVER TWIST

The next evening Nancy overheard Fagin and Monks talking about a lady called Rose who was staying in a hotel in London with Oliver and Mr Losberne. Nancy had a good heart and truly wanted Oliver to have a better life than hers. She hurried to the hotel in the morning and asked to see Rose. It was her only chance to help the young lad, and she would take it if she could.

"I'm about to put my life in your hands," Nancy said. "I am the girl that dragged little Oliver back to Fagin's on the night he left the house in Pentonville."

"You!" said Rose.

"I, lady!" replied the girl. "Do you know a man named Monks?"

"No," said Rose.

"He knows you," Nancy replied, "and he knew you were here – I overheard him say so. Monks saw Oliver accidentally on the day we first lost him at the bookstall. He realised Oliver was the child he had been watching for, though I don't know why. He struck a bargain with Fagin that if he got Oliver back, Fagin should have money. Last night, I heard Monks say: 'The only proofs of the boy's identity lie at the bottom of the river.' Then he said, 'Fagin, you never made such traps as I'll set for my young brother, Oliver.'"

"His brother!" exclaimed Rose.

"Those were his words," said Nancy.

"What should I do? How can I help Oliver?" said Rose. "Where can I find you again if I need you?"

"Every Sunday night, from eleven until twelve," said Nancy, "I will walk on London Bridge if I am alive."

The next day, Oliver, who had been out walking, rushed into the room where Rose sat.

"I have seen Mr Brownlow," he said, "getting out of a coach and going into a house."

"Quick!" she said. "I will take you there directly."

When they arrived, Rose left Oliver in the coach and went in alone. She was presented to two elderly gentlemen.

"Mr Brownlow, I believe, sir?" said Rose.

"That is my name," said one old gentleman. "This is my friend, Mr Grimwig."

"I shall surprise you very much," said Rose, "but you once showed great goodness to a dear young friend of mine: Oliver Twist."

Rose explained everything that had happened to Oliver since he left Mr Brownlow's house.

"Thank God!" said the old gentleman. "This is great happiness to me. But where he is now?"

"He is waiting outside," replied Rose.

She hurried out of the room and returned, accompanied by Oliver.

"There is somebody else who should not be forgotten," said Mr Brownlow. "Send Mrs Bedwin here."

"It is my little boy!" cried the housekeeper, embracing him.

After a happy visit, Rose and Oliver returned home.

The following Sunday night, as the church bell struck eleven, Nancy put on her bonnet.

"Wait!" cried Sikes. "Where's the gal going to at this time of night?"

"I'm not well," said Nancy. "I want a breath of air."

"You won't have it," replied Sikes, suspicious. He rose, locked the door to their home and took the key out.

"Let me go – this minute!" cried Nancy.

"No!" said Sikes. He dragged her, struggling, into a small room, where he held her down by force. She struggled until twelve o'clock had struck, and then gave up.

Soon after, at Fagin's house, Fagin said to one of his gang, Bolter, "I want you to follow a woman. Tell me where Nancy goes, who she sees, what she says."

The next Sunday night, Bill allowed Nancy to leave, and Bolter followed her.

She went to the centre of a bridge, where she stopped. Rose, accompanied by Mr Brownlow, arrived in a carriage, and Nancy made towards them.

"Not here," Nancy said. "Come down these steps!"

Mr Brownlow told Nancy that she must point out Fagin to him.

"I will not!" cried the girl. "I will never do it. He has been good to me!"

"Then," said Mr Brownlow, "I want Monks."

Nancy explained when and where to find Monks, and described him. "He is tall, strongly made; he has a lurching walk; his eyes are sunk deep in his head; upon his throat there is..."

"A broad red mark, like a burn?" cried Mr Brownlow.

"You know him!" said Nancy.

"I think I do," he said.

When they left the bridge, Bolter crept back to Fagin's house and told him all that he had seen and heard.

Later, before daybreak, Fagin sat watching the door as Bolter slept. When Sikes turned up, Fagin hauled Bolter out of bed.

"Tell me again about Nancy, just for him to hear," said Fagin, pointing to Sikes. "How you followed her, and a gentleman and lady asked her to give up all her pals, and Monks first, which she did – and to describe him, which she did – and to tell her where we meet."

"Hell's fire!" cried Sikes. He dashed home and roused Nancy from sleep.

"Bill," said the girl, "why do you look at me like that! Tell me what I have done!"

"You know, you she-devil!" answered Sikes. "You were watched tonight; every word was heard."

"Then spare me!" Nancy cried. "I refused to betray you and Fagin! So spare me!" But Sikes was too angry to listen. He hit her, and she staggered, fell and hit her head. She had time to breathe one last prayer before she died.

When the sun lit up the room where the dead woman lay, Sikes left the house and fled.

That same day, Mr Brownlow found Monks where Nancy said he would be and had him brought to his house.

"Because I was your father's friend," he said, "I will treat you gently now."

"What do you want with me?" said Monks.

"You have a brother, as I believe you know," said Mr Brownlow. "After your father separated from your mother, he fell in love with someone else – Oliver's mother, Agnes. He died before they could marry. I have a portrait of the poor girl." He gestured to the painting on the wall. "When Oliver crossed my path, and I rescued him from a life of vice –"

"What?" cried Monks.

"– and he lay recovering in my house, I saw how much he looked like her portrait. He was snatched away before I knew his history. I thought you might know where to find him and tried to trace you, but until two hours ago I didn't manage to find you.

"You destroyed the proof of Oliver's birth so that he should not inherit any of your father's money. There was a locket that would have shown us who Oliver's mother was, and you got it from Mrs Bumble and dropped it into the river. I've figured you out, Monks."

While Monks was at Mr Brownlow's house, a group of Fagin's robbers were sitting in the upper room of a ruined house.

"When was Fagin took?" one said.

"At dinner time. And the Dodger has been took, too."

There came hurried knocking at the door below. It was Sikes.

"Tonight's paper says that Fagin's took by the police. Is it true?" Sikes said.

"True."

"And – it – Nancy's body – was found?" Sikes asked.

The group nodded.

"It should be buried!" he shouted. "Now, who's that?"

Outside, an angry crowd was gathering. The story of the murder had got out, and everyone knew Sikes must have killed Nancy. The public had come to get him. Sikes opened the window and shouted, "Do your worst! I'll cheat you yet!"

"Give me a rope, a long rope," he cried to one of the robbers. He climbed out of the house and onto the rooftop, planning his escape. But, when the crowd roared upon seeing him, he lost his footing, slipped and fell. That was the last of Bill Sikes.

Two days later, Oliver met with Mrs Maylie, Rose, Mr Brownlow and the man Oliver had seen looking in at the window with Fagin.

Monks cast a look of hate at the astonished boy.

"This child," announced Mr Brownlow, "is Monks' half-brother, the son of his father, by Agnes Fleming, who died giving birth in the workhouse. Tell Oliver, Monks."

Scowling at the trembling boy, the greedy Monks told the whole story again of how he had helped to destroy the documents that left Oliver a share of his father's money, and dropped the locket and ring into the river so that no one should know who Oliver was.

At last, Mr Brownlow turned to Rose.

"Give me your hand," he said gently. "Agnes had a sister, and that sister is Rose. You are Oliver's aunt." Turning to the others, he explained, "Their father died, and Rose lived in poverty until Mrs Maylie saw the girl, pitied her and took her home."

# OLIVER TWIST

The little that remains of Oliver's story can be told in a few words.

The court was packed for Fagin's trial, but not a rustle was heard as the verdict was announced: guilty.

Monks retired to America, where he had a chance to start a new life – but once more he fell into his old ways and ended his life in prison.

Mr and Mrs Bumble had their jobs taken from them and ended up in the very same workhouse that they had once ran.

Rose happily married, and Mrs Maylie moved into Rose and her new husband's happy home.

And Mr Brownlow adopted Oliver as his son, giving Oliver a life as near to one of perfect happiness as can ever be known in this changing world.

# HEIDI

From the village of Mayenfeld, a footpath winds to the foot of the mountains and then upwards. One clear sunny morning in June, two figures were seen walking up it: one a teenage girl, named Dete, the other a child of about four years old, named Heidi. It took them a good hour to walk from Mayenfeld to the village of Dorfli, and it was another hour before they reached Heidi's grandfather's hut.

The hut stood high on the mountainside in full sunshine, with a view of the whole valley beneath. The grandfather had put up a seat outside, and here he was sitting, quietly looking out, when the pair approached. Heidi went straight up to the old man and said, "Good evening, Grandfather."

"What is the meaning of this?" he asked gruffly, giving the child an abrupt shake of the hand and scrutinizing her. Heidi stared at him in return, unable to take her eyes off his long beard and the thick eyebrows that grew together over his nose and looked just like a bush.

"I wish you good day, Uncle," said Dete. "I have brought Heidi, your granddaughter, whom you have not seen since she was a baby. She is to live with you now. I have done my duty looking after her since her mother died, and now it is time for you to do yours."

"That's it, is it?" said the old man. "And what should I do with her when she misses you?"

"That's your business," said Dete, turning on her heel and starting on the path back down the mountain. She felt uneasy about leaving the child with him, so was more rude than she had intended. Still, she told herself, she had no choice. She had a new job in the city of Frankfurt and could not look after Heidi any more.

So Heidi was left high on a mountain with her grandfather, an old man whom she did not know, and who did not know her.

# HEIDI

Grandfather remained seated outside his hut, staring at the ground and smoking his pipe. Heidi explored the goat shed and stared, entranced, at three tall fir trees whose top branches swayed and roared as the breeze blew through them. She then placed herself in front of her grandfather.

"What do you want?" he asked.

"I want to see inside the house," said Heidi.

"Come, then!" he said gruffly.

There was just one large room on the ground floor, with a table, a chair, a bed, a fireplace and a large cupboard where the grandfather kept both his food and his clothes.

"Where am I to sleep?" asked Heidi.

"Wherever you like," he answered.

So Heidi explored further and found a ladder up to the hayloft. There was a large heap of fresh, sweet-smelling hay on the floor and a round window, through which she could see right down the valley.

"I shall sleep here," she called down to him. "It's lovely. Come and see!"

"Oh, I know all about it," he called back, unable to stop himself from smiling.

While Heidi made up her bed, the Grandfather found bread and cheese for them both and toasted it over a cosy fire.

After dinner, Heidi went to bed, calling down, "I like it here, Grandfather!"

Not long after, the grandfather also went to bed. The wind grew so strong during the night that the hut trembled and the old beams groaned and creaked. Around midnight, the old man got up. "The child will be frightened," he murmured half aloud. He climbed the ladder and went to stand by her side. Moonlight was falling through the round window straight onto Heidi's bed.

She lay under the covers, her cheeks rosy with sleep,
her head peacefully resting on her little round arm, and with
a happy expression on her face. The old man stood looking
down on her until the moon disappeared behind the clouds
and he could see no more, then he went back to bed.

# HEIDI

Heidi awoke early the next morning. The sun was shining through the round window, making everything in the loft golden. She climbed quickly down the ladder and ran to the door. Outside, a young goatherd, Peter, was standing with his flock, and Grandfather was bringing his own goats, Little Swan and Little Bear, out of the shed to join them.

"Do you want to go with them on to the mountain?" the grandfather asked Heidi. Nothing could have pleased Heidi better, and she jumped for joy in answer. Grandfather charged Peter with keeping her safe all day and gave him large pieces of bread and cheese for her lunch. Peter opened his eyes wide, for Heidi's lunch was twice the size of his own. Then they were off.

Heidi was enchanted by the mountain: the bright sunshine, the green slopes and all the little blue and yellow flowers. She ran here and there, as lively as the goats themselves, and shouted with delight. Peter had to follow, whistling, calling and gesturing with his stick to get the runaways together again.

At lunchtime, Heidi offered to share her food with Peter. At first he could not believe she was being so kind, but after a minute's hesitation, he thanked her and took it gratefully.

# HEIDI

Later in the day, one of the goats nearly fell down a sheer cliff face, and Peter only just managed to save her. He was frightened and angry and was about to hit her with his stick, when Heidi cried, "No, Peter, you must not hit her. You have no right to touch her!" Peter looked with surprise at the commanding little figure with flashing dark eyes. "Well, I will let her off, if you will give me some more of your cheese tomorrow," he said crossly.

"You shall have it all, tomorrow and every day," replied Heidi. "And bread too. But you must promise never to hit any of the goats."

The bargain was agreed. Heidi was so excited about the mountain and her new life that she chattered all the way back to Grandfather's hut.

# HEIDI

Heidi became so strong and healthy living on the mountain that nothing ever ailed her. She was happy too, as free and light-hearted as a bird.

Winter came, and snow covered the mountain. One clear day, Grandfather got out his sleigh and took Heidi to visit Peter's grandmother, with whom Peter lived, a little way down the mountain. Grandfather left Heidi at Peter's cottage, saying that he would return later.

Peter's cottage was very different from Grandfather's. It was old, shabby and dark, with only two tiny narrow rooms and no bright hayloft above. Heidi introduced herself to Peter's grandmother, an old woman bent with age, then looked around. One of the shutters was flapping in the breeze, filling the tiny room with banging. "Your shutter needs mending," remarked Heidi.

"Yes," said the old woman, "I am not able to see it, but I can hear its sound. The house is falling apart – it worries me so. But there is no one to mend it. Peter doesn't know how."

"Why can't you see it?" asked Heidi.

"Alas, child, I can see nothing. It is always dark for me now."

At this, Heidi started crying. "Can no one make it light for you again?" she sobbed.

"It's all right, child. Your company is doing wonders for me," the old woman said comfortingly. "Come and talk to me. Peter is always out with the goats, so I rarely hear another human voice during the day."

Heidi dried her tears and began to talk about her life on the mountain. "Grandfather will mend your house," she promised.

"I feel the darkness much less when you are with me, Heidi," said the blind grandmother.

When Grandfather collected Heidi, she told him about the grandmother's worries. "We must mend the shutter and other things too," she said. She looked up at him in such trustful confidence that, after a moment, he said, "Yes, Heidi, we will do that; we can mend the shutter if nothing else." And the next day, he was as good as his word.

The seasons rolled on. Heidi learned all kinds of useful things from her grandfather, such as how to look after the goats, but she never went to school. Grandfather wanted her to grow up happy on the mountain; it was dangerous for a young child to travel down to the village school through winter winds, snow and storms, and he had no intention of moving house. Because of his gruff nature, and because he preferred living alone, he did not get on with the villagers.

One day, when Heidi was eight, Aunt Dete came to visit again. She said she had always intended to take the child back to live with her, for she well understood that Heidi must be much in Grandfather's way. And now she had somewhere to take her. Some relatives of the family she worked for had a young daughter, an invalid in a wheelchair, who was lonely. Dete had thought at once of Heidi. She would get an education, Dete said, and who knows what other good fortune might come to her in the future in the big city of Frankfurt?

When Grandfather refused to listen to her idea, Dete was furious.

# HEIDI

"The child knows nothing, and you will not let her learn! When there is such a good opportunity for her as this, only a person who cares for nobody and never wishes good to anyone would think of not jumping at it. You must let her go!"

"Be silent!" thundered Grandfather, his eyes flashing with anger. "Go away and never let me see you again!" And with that he strode out of the hut.

Heidi did not want to leave, but Dete convinced her that Grandfather was angry at both of them and didn't want to see her again. "The city is so nice," she said, "with lots of things to see, and if you don't like it, you can come back again when Grandfather is in a better mood."

Dete bundled Heidi down the mountain, not even allowing her time to say goodbye to the blind grandmother.

# HEIDI

After a long day of travelling, Heidi and Dete arrived in the city and went to the house that was to be Heidi's new home. Clara, the young girl, was lying on a couch waiting for them, and Miss Rottenmeier, the housekeeper who looked after her, was sitting with her. Miss Rottenmeier did not seem pleased to see Heidi, and when she discovered that the girl was only eight years old and could not read, she was furious.

"She is completely inappropriate," she cried angrily. "How can she share school lessons when she cannot read? And Clara is four years older than her. How can she be a proper companion?"

Dete would not be put off, however, and rushed out of the house, leaving Heidi there.

Clara started to tell Heidi about the lessons, about her teacher, who was kind and would surely help Heidi to learn to read, and about how, during the classes, Miss Rottenmeier tried to hide her yawns by covering her face with her handkerchief. "Lessons will be fun now that you are here," she said, and Heidi cheered up slightly.

There were lots of rules to learn in Heidi's new home – about getting up and going to bed, shutting the doors, keeping everything tidy. And when lessons started, she found it impossible to learn the alphabet, though the teacher tried all the ways he could think of to help her. But she and Clara were becoming good friends.

After a week in the city, though, Heidi was homesick for the mountain. She hoped that she would be able to see it from one of the high windows, but all that she could see were the stony streets. Dete had said that she could go home if she didn't like it in the city, but Miss Rottenmeier said she was ungrateful to want such a thing, when she had the best of everything living with Clara. Heidi was miserable. Her only hope was that when Clara's father came home from working away he would let her go.

# HEIDI

Clara's father, Mr Sesemann, arrived late one afternoon. He greeted his daughter affectionately and then held out his hand to Heidi.

"And this must be our little visitor!" he said kindly.

"Yes, Father," said Clara. "Time has passed much more quickly since Heidi has been here, because something fresh happens every day, when it used to be so dull. And we are becoming good friends."

This convinced Mr Sesemann that Heidi should stay with them.

Soon afterwards, Clara's grandmother came to visit. There was something so very kind and warm-hearted about Grandmamma that Heidi felt completely at ease. She had such beautiful white hair and two long ties that hung down from the cap on her head and waved gently about her face every time she moved.

# HEIDI

Grandmamma wanted to help Heidi learn to read. She showed her a pretty picture book, thinking Heidi might like it. Heidi gazed with open-eyed delight at the beautiful pictures, then all of a sudden, as Grandmamma turned over the page, she burst into sobs. The picture showed a green field full of sheep and a shepherd looking after them. "Don't cry, dear child," said Grandmamma. "The picture has reminded you of something. But see, there is a beautiful story to the picture that I will tell you. Dry your eyes, and we will learn to read it together."

Heidi and Grandmamma became very fond of each other, and with the lady's encouragement, Heidi was soon reading very well. But she could not tell Grandmamma how homesick she was. Sadness weighed on her heart; she could not eat; she grew pale and lay awake at night, thinking of home, or weeping quietly so that no one might hear her. Then, one night, Mr Sesemann found Heidi sleepwalking and called in the doctor to advise what was to be done. Heidi admitted her homesickness to the kindly doctor, and it was clear what must happen. Heidi would only be cured if she went home.

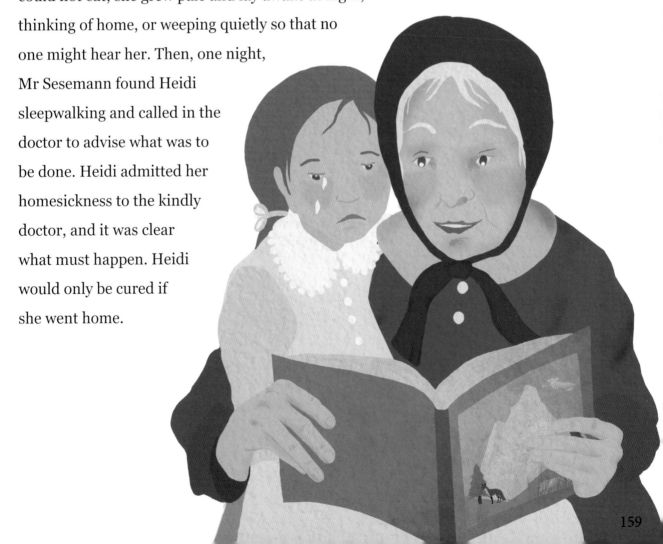

# HEIDI

Heidi was in such a state of excitement when she learned that she was going home that she hardly knew if she was awake or dreaming. Her face glowed rosy with delight as she ran to say goodbye to Clara. Clara was very upset about saying goodbye, but Mr Sesemann promised that he would take her to Switzerland to visit Heidi the next summer. Then it was time to leave. Mr Sesemann wished Heidi a happy journey; she thanked him for all his kindness, and the carriage took her away.

After a long journey, first by train and then by horse and cart, Heidi found herself back in Dorfli. She trembled with excitement, for she knew every tree and rock, and the jagged peak of the mountain looking down on her was like an old friend. Up the steep path she went and at last caught sight of the grandmother's house. She ran faster and faster, her heart beating louder and louder, until she was inside.

# HEIDI

"It is I, Grandmother," she cried, and she flung herself on her knees beside the old woman and clung to her.

The grandmother stroked Heidi's hair and cried tears of joy.

"I am never going away again," said the girl, "and I shall come every day to see you."

She bade the grandmother goodbye and carried on up to Grandfather's hut. When she saw him, Heidi rushed up to him and flung her arms round his neck. He had missed her so much that he started to cry.

"So you have come back to me, Heidi," he said. "Did they send you away?"

"Oh no, grandfather," said Heidi, "but I longed to be home again with you. I used to think I should die, for I felt as if I could not breathe in the city."

There was a shrill whistle, and Peter appeared with his goats. He beamed with pleasure when he saw Heidi and took the hand that she was holding out in greeting. Heidi was home at last.

The next day, Heidi went down the mountain to visit the grandmother as she had promised. The grandmother heard her steps approaching and greeted her as she entered. Then she took hold of Heidi's hand and held it tightly in her own, for she still seemed to fear that the child might be torn from her again.

Heidi caught sight of a hymn book, and a happy idea came to her.

"I can read now," she said. "Would you like me to read you a hymn?"

"Oh, yes," said the grandmother, surprised and delighted. Heidi reached and took the book down from its shelf where it had lain untouched for years. Then she turned the pages until she found a good one.

"Here is one about the sun, Grandmother. I will read you this."

The grandmother sat with folded hands and a look of indescribable joy on her face as Heidi read. "That brings light to the heart!" she said. "What comfort you have brought me!"

"I will come again tomorrow and read to you every day," Heidi promised.

When she got home to Grandfather again, Heidi told him how happy the grandmother was to have hymns read to her. "Everything is happier now than it has ever been in our lives before!" she cried. "If I had come home sooner, as I wanted to, I would not have known how to read, and so I would not have been able to bring comfort to the grandmother in the way I now can. Everything happens for the best, in its own good time, isn't that right, Grandfather?"

Heidi's words played on the old man's mind. He realized that he had been wrong to live so far from Dorfli, so isolated from his fellow men. He also now knew how much he loved Heidi, and how she deserved to live near to other children and go to school like them. So he vowed that when the first snow of winter began to fall, he would close up the hut and take Heidi down to live in Dorfli.

# HEIDI

Heidi was delighted with her new home in Dorfli and enjoyed her first days at school too. On the fourth morning in the village, she said to Grandfather, "I must go up the mountain to see grandmother. It makes her so happy when I read to her."

But Grandfather would not let her go. "The snow is too deep and still falling. You must wait till it freezes, and then you will be able to walk over the hard snow."

When Heidi next visited the grandmother, she found her in bed, trying to keep warm. Heidi read to her, one hymn after another, and a smile of peace spread over the old woman's face.

"Thank you for reading, my child," she said. "No one knows what it is to lie here alone day after day, in silence and darkness, without hearing a voice or seeing a ray of light. When you come and read those words to me, I am comforted."

"If I could read to the grandmother every day," Heidi thought to herself, "then I should go on making her better. But I cannot." Suddenly an idea struck her. Peter must learn to read, so that he could read to the grandmother too!

When she told Peter her idea, he shrugged. "I've tried to learn, but I've never been able to," he said, shamefacedly. "That's why I hate school."

"Well, I will teach you," said Heidi, "and we will start now."

She pulled out a book that Clara had given her and started reading each sentence aloud to him. He then repeated it back to her.

"Good," said Heidi. "If I teach you every evening, and you learn as you have today, you will soon know all your letters."

And so the winter went by, and Peter made real progress, until one evening he was finally able to read to his grandmother. His reading was not perfect – in fact he left out words he found too long or difficult and the grandmother sometimes lost the sense of the hymn – but his intentions were always good.

# HEIDI

Spring came again. The full, fresh streams were flowing down into the valley and clear, warm sunshine lay on the green slopes. After spending the winter in Dorfli, Heidi and her grandfather were back on the mountain for the summer.

One hot day at the end of June a strange-looking procession came up the mountain: a girl being carried carefully by a servant, a stately-looking lady on a horse, an empty wheelchair being pushed by another servant and, finally, a porter carrying a huge bundle of cloaks and shawls. It was Clara and her grandmother, finally coming to visit.

Heidi and Grandfather rushed forwards to meet them, and the two children hugged each other. Grandmamma embraced Heidi, then turned to the grandfather and greeted him warmly. They had heard so much about each other from Heidi in the past that it was as if they were old friends.

Grandfather lifted Clara and sat her gently in her wheelchair, as carefully as if he had looked after her all his life. Then Heidi wheeled her round to see the fir trees, the goat shed and the flowers on the mountain slopes. The wheelchair was too wide to go through the hut's door, so Grandfather lifted Clara again and carried her around to see inside, even taking her up the ladder to Heidi's hayloft bedroom.

Clara was entranced with everything, and her face glowed with excitement at it all. Seeing this, Grandfather said to Grandmamma, "Madam, if you were willing, your granddaughter might stay up here for a little, rather than go back down to Dorfli with you. I am sure she will grow stronger if she stays. We will take great care of her."

"My dear sir," replied Grandmamma, "you give words to the thought that was in my own mind," and she took his hand and gave it a long and grateful shake. Clara and Heidi were overjoyed.

So Clara stayed with Heidi and Grandfather, and slept with Heidi in the hayloft bedroom, lit at night by the moon and stars.

# HEIDI

Clara loved life on the mountain, and Heidi was the best of companions. Grandfather helped Clara to stand a little each day, and, though it hurt her, she made the effort in order to please him.

Every day, Peter had asked Heidi to come on to the mountain with him, but she could not leave Clara. Peter was jealous of Heidi's new friend, and one day his anger boiled over. Seeing the wheelchair outside Grandfather's hut, he pushed it down a steep slope. It fell and smashed on the rocks below. Now Clara would have to leave, he thought.

Indeed, it did seem impossible for Clara to stay. But Heidi had such confidence and happiness in her heart that she believed *anything* was possible. And then, the impossible *did* happen.

Heidi had recently discovered a distant field of flowers, gold, deep blue and sweet-smelling red-brown. She longed for her friend to see it too. Grandfather was not there, and Heidi could not carry Clara alone, so she called Peter to help. Peter was still cross, but he also felt guilty about the wheelchair, so he agreed. Leaning on him, and with Heidi's encouragement, Clara took first one step, then another – and finally she walked to see the flowers!

After that, Clara walked every day. When Grandmamma and Mr Sesemann came to take her back to the city, they were amazed, and their gratefulness to Heidi and Grandfather knew no end. They promised that Clara would come back the following year.

And what of Peter? Grandfather guessed that he had destroyed the chair and thought the boy should be punished. But Grandmamma said kindly to Peter, "What you did was wrong. But if you had not done it, Clara would not have had to make the effort to walk."

Heidi's heart was filled with joy. She was at home with those whom she loved most and who loved her.

"Everything always turns out for the best," she told herself and smiled.

# THE WIZARD OF OZ

Dorothy was an orphan. She lived in a small, one-roomed house in the middle of the vast, treeless Kansas prairies, with her Uncle Henry, who was a farmer, and Aunt Em, Henry's wife. There were no other houses for miles in this bleak, grey landscape.

Uncle Henry and Aunt Em had a big bed in one corner, and Dorothy a little bed in another corner. There was no proper cellar – just a small, dark hole, dug in the middle of the floor, reached by a trapdoor and ladder. This was the cyclone cellar, where the family could go in case one of those great whirlwinds arose, mighty enough to crush any building in its path.

The only thing that kept Dorothy, a merry little girl, from growing as grey as her surroundings was Toto. He was a little black dog with long, silky hair and twinkly black eyes. Dorothy loved him dearly and played with him all day long.

Today, however, they were not playing. Uncle Henry looked anxiously at the sky, as he listened to the low wail of the winds rippling across the flat prairie from the north and south. Suddenly he jumped up.

"There's a cyclone coming, Em," he shouted. "Go to the cellar with Dorothy, and I'll go look after the stock."

One glance at the sky told Aunt Em of the danger close at hand. "Quick, Dorothy!" she cried, as she climbed down the ladder into the small, dark hole.

Dorothy grabbed Toto and started to follow Aunt Em. The house was shaking so hard that she lost her footing and sat down suddenly upon the floor.

A strange thing then happened.

The house whirled around two or three times and rose slowly through the air like a balloon, leaving the prairie and Aunt Em behind. It was caught in the centre of the cyclone, where the wind is still. The pressure of the surrounding wind pushed the house higher and higher, until it was sitting at the very top of the cyclone and was carried miles away.

For hours the house floated on the swirling wind. The swaying motion and darkness were strangely peaceful. Dorothy crawled across the floor with Toto and climbed onto her bed. Soon, with the gentle rocking, she fell fast asleep.

# THE WIZARD OF OZ

Bang! Dorothy woke with a start. The house was no longer moving and sunshine flooded into the little room. She sprang from the bed and, with Toto at her heels, ran outside. With a cry of amazement, Dorothy drank in the beautiful sights that met her eyes: green grass, trees bearing fruits, banks of gorgeous flowers, brightly coloured birds swooping over a gurgling brook.

Out of the corner of her eye, Dorothy noticed a strangely dressed group of people walking towards her. She could tell they were adults, but none of them were taller than Dorothy herself. There were three old men and one much older, white-haired, wrinkly-faced woman.

# THE WIZARD OF OZ

"Welcome, most noble Sorceress, to the land of the Munchkins. We are grateful to you for having killed the Wicked Witch of the East and for setting our people free from her evil rule," said the woman.

Dorothy looked confused. "You're very kind, but I haven't killed anyone."

The woman laughed. "Well, your house did! Look!"

Dorothy turned and saw two legs with ruby slippers on the end of them, sticking out from under a corner of the house.

"Oh, dear!" she cried.

The woman smiled reassuringly. "Don't worry. She was one of the two wicked witches who rule in our Land of Oz. The other lives in the West. I'm the good Witch of the North, and the other good witch rules in the South. But even more powerful than us witches is the Great Oz, a wizard who lives in the Emerald City."

Dorothy felt overwhelmed by all this talk of witches and wizards, and she began to sob. "I must get home to my uncle and aunt," she said. "Can you help me?"

The good witch shook her head. "Only the Great Oz can help you. You must travel to the Emerald City. Oz is a dangerous land, but my kiss will keep you from harm." She kissed Dorothy on the forehead, then handed her the Wicked Witch's ruby slippers. "Wear these. They have special magical powers. And now, just follow the yellow-brick road."

And with that, she disappeared in a puff of smoke.

"Oh!" gasped Dorothy in surprise, and she turned towards the Munchkin men. They bowed low and wished her a pleasant journey before walking away through the trees.

Alone now, Dorothy called to Toto and went into the house to prepare for her journey to the Emerald City. She put on her clean blue-and-white checked dress, took a little basket and filled it with bread, laying a white cloth over the top. Then she looked down at her feet, noticing her old and worn shoes.

"I wonder if these will fit me?" she said, picking up the ruby slippers and remembering the Good Witch's words. The shoes fitted her as if they had been her own.

"Come along, Toto," she said, locking the door of the house. "We'll go to the Emerald City and ask the Great Oz how to get back to Kansas again."

Dorothy began to follow the road paved with yellow bricks. After she had gone several miles, she thought she would stop to rest by a cornfield. Just beyond the fence, she saw a scarecrow, placed high on a pole to keep the birds from the ripe corn.

As Dorothy gazed at the strange painted face, she was surprised to see one of its eyes slowly wink at her. She climbed over the fence to take a closer look.

"Good day," said the Scarecrow in a rather husky voice.

"Did you speak?" Dorothy asked in wonder.

"Certainly!" said the Scarecrow. "I'm not feeling well. If you would be so kind as to help me off this pole, I would feel much better."

Dorothy reached up and lifted the Scarecrow off the pole. Being stuffed with straw, he was quite light!

"Thank you," sighed the Scarecrow. "I feel like a new man! And may I ask who you are, kind young lady? And where are you going?"

"I'm Dorothy," Dorothy replied, and she started to tell the Scarecrow her strange story.

"Who is the Great Oz?" asked the Scarecrow.

"Don't you know?" Dorothy replied in surprise.

The Scarecrow bowed his head sadly. "No. I don't know anything. You see, I'm stuffed, so I have no brains at all."

"Oh," said Dorothy, "I'm awfully sorry for you."

"Do you think," the Scarecrow began, "if I go to Emerald City with you, that Oz will give me some brains?"

"I don't know," replied Dorothy, "but you can come with me, if you like."

The Scarecrow smiled. "I do not want people to call me a fool because my head is full of straw. I don't mind the rest of me being stuffed with straw because I cannot get hurt, but if I don't have a brain, how will I ever know anything?"

Dorothy felt very sorry for the Scarecrow. "If you come with me, I'll ask Oz to do all he can for you."

They walked back to the yellow-brick road.

"Thank you," said the Scarecrow, gratefully. "Let me carry your basket, for I can't get tired."

Dorothy handed her new friend her basket, and they set off on their journey.

# THE WIZARD OF OZ

Towards evening, the travellers came to a great forest. It was dark under the trees, and they stumbled along the path.

"Let's stop if we find a house or somewhere to pass the night," whispered Dorothy.

The Scarecrow stopped. "I can see a little cottage to the left," he said.

He led Dorothy through the trees. The cottage was empty, so they went inside. Dorothy lay down on a bed of dried leaves with Toto and soon fell into a sound sleep. The Scarecrow, who was never tired, stood in a corner and waited patiently for morning.

When Dorothy awoke, the sun was already shining through the trees. After a quick breakfast of bread and a drink of water from a nearby stream, Dorothy called to Toto and the Scarecrow.

"Let's get on our way," she said, anxious to get to the Emerald City as quickly as possible to see if Oz could help her get home again.

They had just stepped onto the yellow-brick road, when they heard a deep groan near by.

"What was that?" Dorothy asked timidly.

"I cannot imagine," replied the Scarecrow. "Shall we go and look?"

They followed the groaning sound back into the forest. Something shiny caught Dorothy's eye, and she stopped with a little cry of surprise.

Standing beside a partly chopped tree, with an uplifted axe in his hands, was a man made entirely of tin. He stood perfectly motionless, as if he could not stir at all.

Dorothy looked at him in amazement.

"Did you groan?" she asked.

"Yes," mumbled the Tin Man, through lips that were nearly rusted together. "I did. I've been groaning for more than a year, and no one has heard me before or come to help me."

Dorothy was moved by the sad voice. "What can I do for you?" she asked softly.

"Go to my cottage over there and get an oil can and oil my joints," he answered. "They are rusted so badly that I cannot move them at all."

Dorothy went into the little cottage. She found the oil can, and, returning quickly, she gently oiled all the Tin Man's joints and his mouth.

"Ah, thank you," he sighed, once he could move again. "You've saved my life. How did you happen to be here?"

"We're on our way to see the Great Oz to ask if he can send me back to Kansas and give the Scarecrow a brain."

The Tin Man appeared to think deeply for a moment. Then he said, "Do you suppose Oz could give me a heart?"

"Why, I guess so," Dorothy answered. "It will be a pleasure to have your company on our journey. But surely, you must already have a heart?"

"Well, I did have a heart once..." replied the Tin Man, and he started to tell his new friends his sad story, as they continued along the path through the forest.

"I was once an ordinary Munchkin boy, and I was in love with a beautiful Munchkin girl. We were going to get married. Unfortunately, the girl lived with an old woman who didn't want her to marry anyone. She was very lazy, and she wanted the girl to remain with her to cook and clean. So the old woman went to the Wicked Witch of the East and got her to cast a spell on me to prevent me marrying the girl."

The Tin Man sighed and then continued. "She enchanted my axe so that it gradually cut off all my limbs and then my head! I went to a tinsmith, and, luckily, he was able to make me new legs, arms and a head out of tin. I could move as long as I kept myself oiled.

"Not satisfied, the Witch made my axe slip and cut my body in two halves. The tinsmith made me a new body, but he couldn't give me a heart. I lost all my love for the Munchkin girl and did not care whether I married her or not.

"One day, I forgot to oil myself. I got caught in a rainstorm and rusted where you found me," finished the Tin Man. "I've had a lot of time to think. While I was in love, I was the happiest man on earth. But no one can love without a heart. If Oz gives me a heart, I will go back to the Munchkin maiden and marry her."

"Let's hope the wizard can help you both," sighed Dorothy, as the Tin Man and Scarecrow chatted on about whether it was better to have a heart or a brain.

Dorothy was just wondering when they'd get out of the forest, when a terrible roar made her stop dead in her tracks. A huge lion bounded onto the path.

With one blow of his huge paw, the Lion sent the Scarecrow spinning over to the edge of the path. Then he struck the Tin Man with his sharp claws. The Tin Man toppled over, but, much to the Lion's surprise, his claws made no marks on the shiny man's body.

Toto started barking and ran towards the Lion. The great beast opened his mouth to bite the little dog, but, before he could snap his jaws, Dorothy, fearing Toto would be killed and heedless of the danger to herself, rushed forwards and slapped the Lion on his nose as hard as she could. The Lion whimpered and started shaking as he backed away.

"Don't you dare bite Toto!" Dorothy screamed. "You ought to be ashamed of yourself, a big beast like you, biting a poor little dog! You're nothing but a big coward!"

"I'm sorry!" cried the Lion, hanging his head in shame. "I try to be brave by acting tough. But it's useless. I can't help being afraid."

"What's happened to make you like this?" huffed Dorothy, as she helped the Tin Man to his feet and patted the Scarecrow back into shape again.

"It's a mystery," replied the Lion. "I'm not brave, even though the lion is supposed to be the King of Beasts. I learned early on that if I roared very loudly, every living thing was frightened and got out of my way."

The Lion wiped a tear from his eye. "If only I could have some courage, my life wouldn't be so unbearable!"

"Perhaps the Great Oz can give you some courage," said the Scarecrow. "Come with us. I'm going to ask him for some brains."

"And I'm going to ask him for a heart," added the Tin Man.

So, once more, the little group set off upon their journey. What adventures the friends had that day while travelling through the forest! They had to flee from many strange creatures and cross huge ditches that blocked their path on the yellow-brick road.

Finally, they came to a broad river at the edge of the forest. Dorothy feasted on nuts and fruit before curling up with Toto. Feeling safe with her new band of friends, she fell fast asleep.

Dorothy and her friends awoke the next morning refreshed and full of hope. The Tin Man made a raft from logs for them to cross the broad river.

They climbed onto the raft, and things were going well until they reached the middle of the river. The swift current swept the raft downstream, further and further away from the yellow-brick road on the other side.

"Oh, what a disaster!" cried the Scarecrow. "We must get to the Emerald City." He put his pole into the water to try and stop the raft, but it got stuck. The Scarecrow was left clinging to the pole in the middle of the river, while the raft with the others floated off without him.

"Oh, no, what are we going to do?" cried Dorothy.

"Hold onto my tail," cried the Lion, as he jumped into the river, "and I'll swim to shore with the raft."

After a hard struggle, the Lion reached the shore.

"We must get back to the yellow-brick road and save the Scarecrow," said Dorothy.

Suddenly, they saw the Scarecrow. A kind stork had lifted him from his pole in the river and was dropping him on the bank by a field of poppies.

The friends were delighted and set off through the poppy field.

"I feel so sleepy," yawned the Lion.

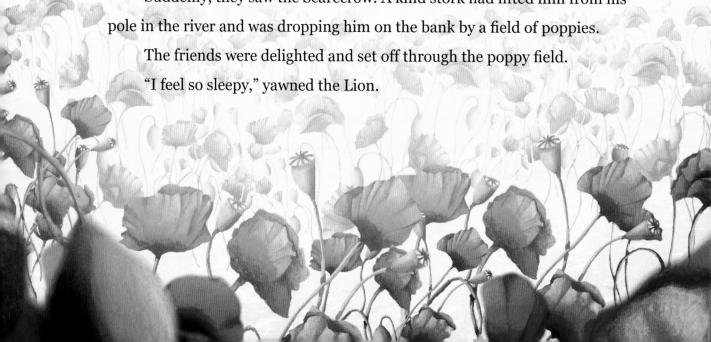

"Me too!" whispered Dorothy. "The smell of these flowers is too much…"

She swayed and then suddenly dropped to the ground. Within seconds, the Lion and Toto fell next to Dorothy. They were soon all fast asleep. Only the Tin Man and the Scarecrow were left standing.

"It must be these flowers," cried the Tin Man. "Quick, help me carry them away from here." The two friends realized that the flowers were poisonous to humans and animals.

As they were trying to work out how they could carry the heavy Lion, a large wildcat raced past them, chasing a field mouse. Without thinking, the Tin Man struck out with his axe, killing the wildcat immediately.

"Thank you so much!" squeaked the mouse. "You saved my life. I'm the Queen of the Field Mice. Is there anything I can do for you?"

"We need to get our friend the Lion out of this field," said the Tin Man. "Can you help us?"

The Queen summoned all her mice, and they helped the travellers pull the sleeping Lion out of the field.

"Thank you for helping us," cried the Tin Man.

"You saved my life," replied the Queen. "If you ever need us again, just call out, and we will come to your assistance. Goodbye!"

As soon as Dorothy, Toto and the Lion woke up, the travellers continued on their journey.

When they finally reached the Emerald City, they saw a huge wall surrounding the city. Amidst its dazzling emeralds, they found a big gate. Dorothy rang the bell next to it. The gate swung open, and they all passed through.

# THE WIZARD OF OZ

A little man stood before them, dressed in green.

"What do you wish in the Emerald City?" he asked.

"We came here to see the Great Oz," replied Dorothy.

The man stared at Dorothy. "I am the Guardian of the Gates. If you wish to see the Great Oz, I must take you to his Palace."

Dorothy and her friends were shown to rooms in the palace and were told they would be collected, one by one, to see Oz.

Dorothy was the first to be taken to the wizard's Throne Room. Above a chair in the middle of the room floated a giant head. Dorothy gazed upon it in wonder and fear.

"I am Oz, the Great and Terrible. Who are you, and why do you seek me?" said the floating head.

Nervously, Dorothy replied, "I am Dorothy, the Small and Meek. I have come to you for help." And she told Oz her story.

The floating head nodded. "Before I can help you, you must kill the Wicked Witch of the West. Now go, and do not ask to see me again until you have done your task."

With a heavy heart, Dorothy went back to her friends and told them what had happened. One by one, the Tin Man, Scarecrow and Lion were all told the same thing by the great wizard.

"What shall we do now?" weeped Dorothy.

"There is only one thing we can do," replied the Lion. "We must seek out the Wicked Witch and destroy her!"

# THE WIZARD OF OZ

The next day, Dorothy and her friends left the dazzling Emerald City, following the advice of the gatekeeper: "Keep to the West, where the sun sets, and you cannot fail to find the Wicked Witch."

The Wicked Witch of the West had eyes as powerful as a telescope, and she could see everywhere in the land. She spied the little group of friends and was angry to find them in her country.

"I will destroy them," she cackled, and, with a blast upon a silver whistle, she summoned a pack of fierce wolves.

The wolves attacked the travellers, but the brave Tin Man, wielding his axe, killed them all, saving his friends.

The Witch was furious. With another blast of her whistle she sent a flock of vicious crows to attack the little group. This time the courageous Scarecrow fought and killed all the crows. She stamped her feet in anger.

"I will summon the Winged Monkeys with the power of the Golden Cap," she screeched. "This time they will not escape!"

The Golden Cap was charmed, and whoever owned it could call three times upon the Winged Monkeys to help them.

The Winged Monkeys were too powerful for the little band of travellers, and the friends were captured and taken to the Witch's castle.

When the Witch saw the Good Witch of the North's kiss of protection on Dorothy's forehead, even she was afraid to touch the girl. Instead, she forced

Dorothy to work in the kitchen of her castle, cooking and cleaning, and plotted how to get the magic ruby slippers that Dorothy still wore on her feet.

Several weeks went past. Then, one day, the Witch tripped Dorothy over as she was cleaning the kitchen floor, and Dorothy lost one of her shoes. The Witch grabbed it. "Soon the other one will be mine!" she cackled gleefully.

Dorothy was furious. "You are a wicked creature!" she screamed at the Witch. "You have no right to take my shoe from me."

The Witch just laughed, which made Dorothy even angrier. Dorothy picked up the bucket of water next to her and threw it over the Witch.

"No! See what you have done!" screamed the Witch. "In a minute I shall melt away!"

Dorothy watched in horror as the Witch disappeared into a puddle of water. With a trembling hand, Dorothy grabbed the ruby slipper from the puddle, which was all that remained of the Witch, and put it on. Then she raced out of the kitchen to find her friends.

With much joy in their hearts, Dorothy and her friends set free everyone the Witch had enslaved over the years.

Before they left the castle, Dorothy went to the Witch's cupboard to fill her basket with food for the journey back to Oz. Lying on one of the shelves was the Golden Cap. Dorothy picked it up.

"This is pretty," she said, putting the Cap on. It fitted her perfectly, so she decided to keep it – after all, the Witch wouldn't need it now! Dorothy, however, didn't know it had magical powers.

With her basket full, Dorothy and her friends began their return journey to the Emerald City.

"I shall get my brains!" cried the Scarecrow.

"I shall get my heart!" laughed the Tin Man.

"I shall get my courage!" roared the Lion.

"And I shall get back to Kansas!" sighed Dorothy, clapping her hands.

Days went by, and the travellers began to wonder if they would ever get back to the Emerald City. They couldn't see the yellow-brick road any more, just field after field disappearing into the distance.

"We have surely lost our way," grumbled the Scarecrow. "I shall never get my brains now."

Dorothy sighed. "We could call the field mice." She turned to the field, shouting at the top of her voice, "Dear mice, please help us!"

Within a few minutes, an army of small mice appeared. "We've lost our way," Dorothy explained.

The Queen mouse looked at Dorothy. "The City is a great way off. Why don't you use the charm of the Cap and call the Winged Monkeys? They will carry you there in less than an hour."

"What charm?" queried Dorothy.

The Queen explained, and soon Dorothy and her friends were being carried back to the Emerald City by the Winged Monkeys.

# THE WIZARD OF OZ

After the friends had been back in the Emerald City for over a week, the wizard still refused to see them.

"I'm going to find out what is going on," said Dorothy, and she ran past the guard into the wizard's palace. Sitting in the vast throne room was a small, old man. Dorothy was crushed. There was no Great Oz. He was just an ordinary man.

"I'll never get home now," sobbed Dorothy. "You broke all your promises!"

"I'm truly sorry," sighed the little old man. He gestured to Dorothy's friends to join him, and he told them his story. He used to work in a circus in the city of Omaha. One day, the hot-air balloon he was in accidentally floated away. When it eventually landed in Oz, the people thought he was a great wizard, and he was too scared to tell them otherwise.

"Can't you give me brains?" asked the Scarecrow.

"You don't need them. You are learning something every day," said Oz. "Look at yourselves, all of you, you have already got what you are seeking – brains, heart and courage. You've stuck by each other and helped each other and given each other the love of friendship."

The Tin Man, Scarecrow and Lion looked at each other and smiled.

"But how will I get home?" whispered Dorothy.

"You must go to see Glinda the Good Witch of the South," Oz replied.

"Dorothy, you have helped us get what we wanted and made us so happy," said the Tin Man. "We will help you find Glinda."

So, once again, the group of friends set out on another long and difficult journey. But with their new-found courage, love and knowledge, they finally arrived at Glinda's palace.

Dorothy told the Good Witch her story.

Glinda leaned forwards and kissed the little girl before her. "All you have to do is knock the heels of your ruby slippers together three times and command them to carry you wherever you wish to go," she said.

Dorothy hugged her friends tightly.

"Thank you," she whispered. "I'll never forget you." And with tears in her eyes, she clicked her heels three times.

"Take me home to Aunt Em!"